In Front of Me

A Simple Love Story: Book 4

Dana LeCheminant

Cover design copyright © 2020 by Sheridan Bronson
Cover image © 2020 by AllaSerebrina/Depositphotos.com
Utensil element © 2020 by Vecteezy.com

This book is a work of fiction. The characters, names, incidents, places, and dialogue are either products of the author's imagination or are used fictitiously. Any resemblance to actual persons, living or dead, events, or locales, is entirely coincidental.

First Printing: June 2020

ISBN: 978-1-951753-04-7

for Sheri: thanks for brainstorming, listening, designing, and loving my characters as much as I do

CHAPTER ONE

December 2018

When Seth called for the third time in as many minutes, I knew I wasn't going to be able to ignore my brother today. And that made my stomach hurt as I considered my ever-growing list of things I had to do. He was never this persistent—he knew I rarely answered my phone during work hours—which meant whatever he was calling to talk to me about, it was something important. And Seth Hastings didn't take importance lightly.

Could he have picked a worse time, though?

Sighing, I picked up my phone and hovered over the answer button for a moment before I connected the call and held the phone to my ear.

"So you are alive," he said before I even took a breath to greet him.

I winced. He was literally on the other side of the country, and he still managed to put me on edge with his growl. If I didn't know he was one of the kindest, sweetest men on the planet, I might have believed his anger. But it was really just a mask, and he was using it on me for the first time in a long time. I didn't like that. "Nice to talk to you too," I muttered, and my eyes returned to my computer screen.

I still had a presentation to prepare, and if my assistant, Travis, didn't come back soon with the report I'd sent him for, I was going to have a whole lot of nothing to show the firm's board. It didn't matter how good of a financial analyst I was; I had to prove I was worth the consideration for the promotion. *Someone* had to lead the team, and I wasn't going to let Cal Mikaelson pass me over yet again. This was my year.

"Would you stop working for two minutes, Lissa?" Seth grumbled into the phone. Either he was a better super soldier than I thought and had somehow managed to set up surveillance in my office, or my half-brother knew me a little too well for a guy I'd only met a few years ago.

"I don't know what you're talking about," I said and pulled up my projection sheet for Sonya Yun's portfolio. This info was a start, but I needed Travis to come back with that report. Without it, this was just a bunch of numbers. "Was there something you needed, Seth?"

"Yeah," he replied. "I need you to stop working for two minutes so I can know you're actually paying attention and not just tuning me out while you browse stock markets."

I rolled my eyes, even if he couldn't see me. I figured he could probably sense my annoyance, since he was pretty much superhuman. It was a pity he had given up his Special Forces days to be a private bodyguard; his skills were a bit wasted on the quiet life he lived now. "You clearly have no idea what I do for my job," I said. "Which is rich, coming from a guy who has a degree in Economics."

"Not the point," he replied.

I quickly sent yet another message to my assistant, asking him where he was and why it was taking him over an hour to go two floors down and grab a folder. "But seriously, Seth," I said, "I have to get back to work. What is this about?"

"I'm getting married on Saturday, Liss."

I nearly dropped my phone. *This* Saturday? But his wedding wasn't until December. I had a whole... I stared at the calendar on my wall, realizing with a twist in my stomach that it *was* December.

"That's what I thought," Seth said, apparently reading into my silence. "You forgot about Thanksgiving—again—so I figured I would give you a reminder for this one. I'm only getting married once."

If you're lucky, I thought to myself. I had no reason to doubt his marriage would be a lasting one, since his fiancée, Catherine, was quite possibly the most perfect woman in the world, but I had seen love fall apart—especially in my own life—way too many times to not be a bit cynical.

"I didn't forget your wedding," I lied.

"So you'll be here?"

If I got this promotion, which was the plan and had been for years,

I was going to have to dive right in and completely overhaul the whole department to get it running smoothly. And that wasn't something I could do overnight. I couldn't just drop everything and leave Boston for a whole weekend.

"Seth," I said and braced myself for his disappointment. There was nothing about my brother that was small—physically or emotionally—and he wouldn't bother hiding his feelings from me just because he was all the way in California. He would probably even exaggerate them to make me feel worse than I already did.

But he surprised me, hitting me with a long stretch of silence instead of a complaint or reproach, and when he did speak, he did it quietly, keeping his deep voice as soft as he could make it. "Look," he said. "I know you don't know what it was like growing up with Dad."

I wasn't even going to grace that statement with a comment. Seth could call the man "Dad" all he wanted, but Gordon Hastings was no father to me. Even if our shared DNA said otherwise. The man had been pretty clear about how he felt about our familial ties to each other. As in there weren't any.

"But I know you know how important family is," Seth continued. "And this new family of mine—Catherine's family—is the best there is. I couldn't share my dad with you, so please let me share the Davenports. I don't want you to be alone for the rest of your life."

It was a sweet gesture, but that didn't change the fact that my life plans hinged on this meeting today. The meeting I was already late for. "Seth," I said again and wished I could give him better news. "Work is crazy right now. I wish I could leave, but I…"

He sighed. "Fine," he said. "But I bought you a plane ticket anyway. Just in case." He hung up before I could say anything, and my chest grew tight.

What a terrible sister I was.

Before I could work up the nerve to call him back and try to explain, Travis *finally* pushed through my office door, out of breath and looking like he had just run straight into a lion's den and wanted to be anywhere but here. The expression wasn't surprising, but his empty hands were.

"Travis," I said, catching the way he flinched when I said his name. "Where's my report?"

The poor kid swallowed, apparently terrified. That didn't help alleviate the uneasiness building inside me. "Well…"

"You said Jennings got it done."

"He did."

"So where is it?"

Glancing around the office seemed to give him some strength and straighten his stature, though his courage waned again when he looked at me. He hunched his shoulders back to where they'd been before, and he took a backward step toward the door. Ready to run. "Because he gave it to Hamada," he whispered.

I jumped to my feet fast enough that Travis leapt for the door and was halfway out by the time I said, "He did *what?* Hamada's been here for two months. He shouldn't be authorized to even *see* that report."

Glancing down at the phone in his hand, Travis looked very much like a little rodent stuck in a trap and trying to free himself from the glue. "Did I not send you the memo?" he asked so quietly I barely heard him. "Hamada was promoted."

Which meant I had yet another rung to climb on the ladder. This meeting, this presentation, was supposed to give me an extra boost to the top, and some freshly made college grad had—yet again—pulled the rug out from under me right before I made the jump. How was I supposed to go anywhere if all of my plans kept getting derailed by imbeciles?

I was *so* glad I chose to wear heels today. I needed to be tall.

The instant I was outside my office, the whole floor went silent, and I could feel every man's eyes on me as I went, though I tried to ignore them. It wasn't like I *wanted* to scare the file clerk every time I stormed past his desk on my way to Mikaelson's office, which happened far more often than it should have. I kept waiting for the day he didn't see me in time to hide and couldn't avoid the full brunt of my glare, therefore keeling over dead right where he sat. The others beyond him were never any less intimidated than the clerk, and poor Travis would likely only last a few more weeks before I put him under enough stress that he quit. I didn't want to do it, but I had to.

In a world full of men, a woman like me could show no weakness.

"You promoted Hamada to team leader?" I asked, pushing past Mikaelson's assistant into his office. "Have you gone insane?"

Cal Mikaelson was the sort of man who had all the power he could possibly need and still craved more, and he was the one person at this stupid company I hadn't yet been able to intimidate. He just sat there in his thousand-dollar ergonomic chair and played with the signed baseball he held in his hands, a smug grin on his ridiculous face.

"Lissa," he greeted, almost laughing my name. "Hamada is smart."

"As smart as a twelve-year-old, maybe," I argued. "That was supposed to be *my* job. *My* team."

"Don't get your pencil skirt in a twist, sweetheart."

"Don't even start," I snarled, my stomach clenching and unnecessarily reminding me why I hated this man in front of me. He did that often enough on his own.

"Hamada has the same fancy degree you have," Mikaelson continued, completely ignoring my anger. "But he has a more innovative mind. He's more in the know about what's going on with the new adult generation, so he understands that millennial sense of mind that you just can't grasp. It's not your fault."

My fingers curled into fists, and I wondered if I could shove that baseball down his throat or if using it as a murder weapon would only increase its value. "I'm only twenty-eight," I said. "And I have *years* of experience over Hamada."

Rising, he set his baseball on its special little stand then gave me an examining look like he always did as he headed for the door. "You're just not cut out for that extra level of stress, sweetheart," he said. "Go cry into a pillow and get over it."

That was it.

"I quit," I replied.

He froze in the doorway. "What did you just say?"

This was a terrible mistake, but it was too late now. The words came rushing out of my mouth as if they'd been teetering at the edge for a long time. They probably had. "You heard me," I said. "Good luck getting that mess of children to do their jobs without me *breathing down their necks*, as they like to say behind my back."

I'd never seen the man's face so red, and I had to fight a smile when I realized I had actually ruffled the guy's feathers for the first time in four years. "I'll consider this your two weeks'," he growled.

I kept my head high, though it suddenly felt like the roof was collapsing over me. It had taken me two years to get this job. Another year to get myself to this level, where I'd been fighting ever since to climb higher. If I left now, I would have to start all over in another office full of men who would be convinced no woman had any business being a financial analyst. Maybe if I... *No.* I needed to leave. Staying wasn't worth it.

Besides, I had a wedding to attend. Had Seth known something like this would happen, or was he just painfully optimistic? It was probably a mixture of both. But whatever reasons he had for buying me that plane ticket, I was just glad I didn't have to pay for it myself.

Without a job, my life—and in turn my bank account—was about to spiral out of control.

But there was more to life than fighting for a place at a table no one wanted me at, right? It was time to find something new, even if that meant throwing all of my plans and goals down the drain. "I'll be using my paid time off for the next two weeks," I said. "I wish I could say it has been a pleasure, but…" I strode past him as he flexed his fist, the threat of lawsuit the only thing keeping him from grabbing my arm in anger like I knew he wanted to.

"You can't do that," he snarled.

I didn't even look back, knowing that if I did, my threadbare confidence would snap. "Try to stop me."

CHAPTER TWO

I used to like weddings. I used to watch as a happy couple said their vows and promised to love each other forever before sharing the most perfect kiss. Like any normal girl, I had my own wedding planned down to the color of flowers and what sort of shoe my bridesmaids would wear, both of which varied by season. Love—the whole reason weddings even existed—gave me hope for the future.

And then I grew up.

It wasn't like I no longer believed in love. I saw it every day, in a man holding his wife's purse while she tried on a jacket and a little note left in a lunch brought from home and those looks that two people shared when they had a joke only they understood. Love was all around me, but it wasn't something I could imagine for myself. It just didn't fit into the plan.

"Not anymore."

"What was that?"

Best not to talk to myself while surrounded by my brother's new family. They were all having the time of their lives at the reception, and I had been doing everything I could not to draw attention my way. Talking to myself was the exact opposite of what I wanted to be doing, and I winced when I realized it was Indie who had heard my muttered comment. As the Maid of Honor, she'd spent a whole lot of energy on me already, pretending we were the best of friends and making it impossible for me to disappear into a corner and research jobs on my phone.

"Nothing," I said and tugged at the fabric of my bridesmaid dress as I sat in a luxurious banquet hall wishing I was anywhere but here. I hadn't even *agreed* to be a bridesmaid, but my new sister-in-law, Catherine, was persistent, just like her husband. She'd probably known as well as Seth did that I would end up here in California, so she'd planned everything as if I had been just as eager as Indie to be a part of this. Okay, so the ceremony had been nice, and the food was amazing, so I couldn't complain *too* much. But did the dress have to be so tight?

Scooting closer to me, Indie looped her arm through mine and gave me a grin. "Having fun?" she asked, and I was pretty sure she was entirely aware that I was planning an early escape. If I got myself back to Seth and Catherine's apartment, I could grab my stuff and be on a red-eye flight back to Boston. I really needed to get started on the job hunt, unless I wanted to get kicked out of my apartment before I even had a chance to fully pack.

For a girl with not one but *two* degrees from an Ivy League school, one of those in finance, I would have thought I would be better at money management and have more of a savings built up. Maybe if Cal had actually promoted me when I planned instead of pushing it back year after year until I finally snapped…

"Seth was right," Indie said with a laugh, pulling my focus back to her. "You have a hard time paying attention to what's in front of you."

I shot a glare at my brother, who was off dancing with Catherine, but he was a little preoccupied by his new wife to notice me. Geez, they looked happy. It should have been illegal for two people to be so blissfully in love. "Has he been telling the whole family my life story?" I wondered out loud. It didn't matter that he was right; I didn't know these people, and I had a feeling they would try to smooth out all my rough edges if given the chance. Seth didn't need to be making his family pity me.

"He's been telling anyone who would listen that his sister is a lot cooler than she seems at first glance," someone else replied.

This time I turned my glare to Matthew Davenport, Catherine's cousin and Indie's boyfriend, but he just laughed as he watched Seth and Catherine dance. "That's a compliment, Lissa," he said and raised his eyebrows, and then he was on his feet. "Now if you'll excuse me, I think the dance floor is finally opening up for competitors. Indie, my love? Shall we show these losers how it's done?"

Rolling her eyes, Indie waved him off and said, "Be there in a minute, you big idiot." When Matthew hurried off to steal Catherine from

Seth for the next dance, Indie pulled her arm free from mine but stayed close. She watched them for a moment, a grin on her face as Matthew and Catherine laughed while they danced. Seth had begun dancing with his mom just beyond them, though he barely took his eyes off his wife. "He's a good man, isn't he?" Indie asked.

"Which one?" I replied.

"Both. But I meant Seth. He's good for Catherine, and you're lucky to have him as a brother."

Boy, did I know it. Not for the first time, I wished I'd had him as a brother for longer than I had. I didn't even meet the guy until I was at Yale, and it took several months for us to realize we shared a father. I really was happy for him, even if I wasn't good at showing it, and this wedding was the most beautiful thing I'd ever been a part of. My brother never went small, and this whole thing was a perfect blend of him and Catherine. "He's the best brother a girl could ask for," I admitted. "Not to mention I will never fear for my life. Ever."

Indie's laugh, though not particularly loud, caught Matthew's attention, and he nearly tripped over Catherine's extravagant dress when he smiled at his girlfriend. "Yes," she agreed as she tried not to laugh harder, "Seth is quite the…man."

That was one way of putting it. Seth was a giant. Two hundred and fifty pounds of muscle packed into more than six and a half feet, he was definitely a force to be reckoned with. There was a reason most of the world was afraid of the man who'd spent the last several years working secret ops with the US Special Forces. But for all his impressive exterior, he was absolutely the nicest, sweetest person I'd ever known. He was lucky he'd found Catherine, and I envied him for that happily ever after.

My life had never been a fairy tale, and that wasn't likely to change anytime soon.

"Anyway," Indie said with a cough, "I just wanted to make sure you don't feel neglected. It took me a while to feel comfortable around this family, so I get it."

And now I felt bad for being grumpy. "No, that's not—"

"If you need anything, just let me know," she said, and then she jumped up and hurried into Matthew's arms after he handed Catherine back to her new husband.

She meant well. And technically I *was* part of the family now that Seth had married into the Davenports. I may have been a Hastings by blood, thanks to the absent father I shared with Seth, but in reality, I was a Montgomery, raised by a mother who worked two jobs and spent countless hours studying with me and tutoring me to help get me to Yale. I worked for every penny I had, and the longer I stayed, the more these people would realize I was not actually one of them.

I sighed, running my finger along the edge of my water glass and making it ring, and I dropped my head into my other hand as I returned to making plans to leave early. A last-minute flight change would cost me more, so I had to make sure it was really worth it. I was already going back tomorrow, so would that one extra day really benefit me? If it meant I wouldn't have to endure any more of this sickeningly happy event, it probably would.

"I know that look," a deep voice said beside me, and I grimaced.

Putting on my best smile, I turned and said, "Hey, Seth."

My brother smiled back, but there was an undercurrent of worry in his eyes that meant he knew exactly what I was thinking about. "You're really going to sneak out of my wedding without saying goodbye?" he asked.

There was little point in lying. "I'm exhausted," I said and hoped that would be enough. I was sure if I told him about leaving my job, he would understand, but I wasn't ready for him to try to fix that for me. I could take care of myself well enough, and his immediate attempts to help would only make me more humiliated about the whole thing than I already was. "I think I just need to go to bed early," I told him. "You should go back to your wife."

Though he glanced at Catherine, who was dancing to an upbeat song with her cousin Lanna now, Seth shook his head and held out his massive hand to me. "Nope," he said. "I want to dance with you." It wasn't an order, but he certainly made it sound like one. You could take the man out of the military, but you couldn't take the military out of the man. "Come on, Liss. Just one song."

Groaning, I considered my options for only a moment before I put my hand in his and let him pull me to my feet as the song changed to something calmer than the last. He maneuvered us to the dance floor and directed me into a spin before pulling me into his arms, and then he grinned.

"Is this so bad?" he asked as we slowly rotated to the music.

I had to admit, he made it easy to follow his steps, and dancing with him felt more normal than anything had in the last few days. I forced a smile then dropped my head onto his shoulder and let out a sigh. I may have only known him for a few years, but I had always been completely comfortable around my brother. He had a way of reminding me that I didn't have to fight to impress the people who mattered.

"What's wrong?" he asked. He didn't sound worried, though. Simply sympathetic.

I wanted to tell him everything, but I wasn't about to ruin his wedding day. "Nothing," I said. *Just all my life plans have gone to pot.*

"You keep telling yourself that." After a few blissfully quiet seconds, during which we just swayed a bit to the music, he muttered, "Sorry I haven't had much of a chance to talk to you since you got here."

I would have rolled my eyes if I hadn't shut them when I rested my head against him. I just wanted to go to bed, and Seth had a way of blocking out the rest of the world and making me feel safe. "It's your wedding, Seth," I said. "Of course you're going to be busy."

"Has my family been welcoming?" he asked next, and I could hear the worry in his voice. He had tried more than once to get me to fly out to California to meet Catherine's cousins, and I had found excuses every time. A good chunk of that was because of work, but also, I hadn't wanted to intrude. This was his new family, not mine.

"They've been great," I said, even if they were almost *too* nice. Catherine's cousin Lanna, the third bridesmaid, and her husband, Adam, had constantly asked if I was hungry or if I needed some water or a place to take a nap, and Matthew had spent the whole drive from the airport this morning asking me questions about my life back east. With Indie's not-so-subtle comments just a few moments earlier, as well as every bit of attention she'd given me the rest of the day, I was about ready for a break from the ridiculously accommodating Davenports. But I had to make sure Seth didn't get it into his head that something was seriously wrong, so I added, "I'm still not sure how you managed to convince them you were normal enough to be one of them."

Seth laughed, and the sound rumbled in my ear. "I don't know if you know this about me," he said, "but I can be exceptionally persuasive when I want to be."

"It's pronounced 'pigheaded,'" Matthew said, and I opened my eyes just as he and Indie danced past then disappeared into the crowd before Seth could retaliate.

I grinned when I caught sight of my brother's glare. "I think you found your match in your new cousin-in-law," I said, knowing he would hate the idea of someone not being afraid of him.

"Matthew's lucky I like him," Seth grumbled back, but his smile returned pretty quickly. "I'm glad you came, Lissa. Seriously."

As difficult as it was to be here surrounded by so much love and happiness when I was in the middle of a quarter-life crisis, I made myself return his smile. "So am I," I said, and I mostly meant it. I didn't get to spend nearly enough time with my brother. "But I would love to sit down before my feet fall off. Catherine has great taste in shoes, but I'm not sure she knows how to pick comfortable ones."

Chuckling, Seth brought me to the edge of the dance floor and gave me a little bow that made me snort a laugh. "Beauty is pain," he agreed then thankfully left me on my own so he could return to the rest of the Davenports. His family.

It would be the perfect time to make my escape, but suddenly I couldn't bring myself to do that to Seth. He clearly wanted me to share this day with him, and how could I ignore that when he was the best brother in the world? Sighing, I returned to my table so I could wallow a bit before I tried to be a better sister and actually be a part of the celebration. I could do that for one night, and then I would fly back to an apartment I could no longer afford before anyone decided to take pity on the girl who had no business being in their lives.

"It hurts, doesn't it?"

"Yeah," I sighed. Then I froze. Turned. And I stared at the unfamiliar man who had slipped into the vacant seat next to me without me even noticing. "Sorry, what?"

He smiled, the little lights overhead reflecting off his perfect teeth, and he leaned a bit closer, one elbow on the table and a watch on his wrist that cost half my rent. "Knowing you're missing out on something spectacular by not coming over and talking to a guy like me," he said.

Oh, the poor thing. "Has that line ever worked for you?" I asked. I was too tired to play games, and I'd encountered his type more times than I could count. It was one of the downsides of having Gordon Hastings as a father. Being his daughter meant I was generally considered pretty, and therefore guys like this one flocked to me at events like this without ever bothering to get to know me. I was just a face to them.

The man at my side simply laughed, settling against the back of his chair and keeping his steely blue eyes locked on me. "I've got a zero percent success rate at this point," he replied, "though I think I need a little more data before I throw it out completely. Once just isn't enough to really tell if it works. But thank you for participating in my survey." Then he gave a little bow and held out his hand. "I'm Brennon Ashworth."

I really didn't want to indulge him, but he was charming. I'd give him that. "Lissa Montgomery," I replied and grasped his hand.

"Ah, the Hastings reject."

Whoa now. Instantly on the defense, I pulled my hand back and assumed the business face that generally made Travis take an early lunch. "Well aren't you a charmer?" I grumbled.

Brennon grinned again. "I meant it as a compliment," he assured me, looking out over the crowd of people dancing. The people of California really needed to figure out how compliments worked—he was no better than Matthew. "Seth doesn't like being a Hastings any more than I'm sure you do."

"So you're on the groom's side," I surmised. Funny how Seth never mentioned he had a particularly handsome single friend. There had to be a reason for that. *What's wrong with you, Brennon Ashworth?*

"Bride's side, technically," Brennon corrected. "Catherine is certainly stunning tonight, isn't she?"

"Don't let Seth hear you say that."

He turned to face me again, his smile bringing out a slight increase in my heart rate. I was too tired to not be affected by a look like that. "You're stunning too," he said. "How much trouble do you think I'd be in if Seth heard me say *that?*"

A large part of me hoped he'd be in a lot of trouble. It was nice to know I had someone looking out for me. Offering up my own wide—albeit exhausted—smile, I said, "You probably shouldn't take your chances," and reached for the untouched cheesecake Matthew had left on the table.

Brennon grabbed my hand before I could. "You're not going to believe me when I say this," he said, "but I really don't do this."

I looked at his fingers wrapped around mine and raised an eyebrow, pleased when he immediately let go. "You don't stop women from enjoying dessert?"

His little laugh was almost adorable as he fought to keep his smile. "I know this is going to sound like I'm some frat boy," he said, "and

I'm fully owning that unfortunate comparison, even if it's wildly untrue. But I don't walk up to beautiful women I've never met and hope they give me the time of day." At some point he'd leaned reasonably close to me, and I hadn't even noticed.

"And why is that?" I asked quietly, as if we had some deep secret to share with each other. Mostly I just wanted him to leave me alone to my misery, but he was cute.

He frowned, as if thinking about how he wanted to answer my question. When he did speak, he did so hesitantly. "Because I don't believe in love," he said, "so I don't usually bother."

That…that wasn't what I expected. "You mean love at first sight?" I asked.

He winced as he sat up and brought a bit of distance back between us. "Love in general. I'm really selling myself, aren't I?" He muttered something under his breath and looked thoroughly disappointed in himself.

I had to process that, which wasn't easy when that disappointment made him all the more attractive. "Everyone believes in love," I argued. "How could you not when you're stuck watching those dorks all day?" I added, waving toward the Davenport family as all six of them did some weird line dance together and looked absolutely ridiculous.

Brennon followed my gesture, and the moment he looked away, a cough pulled my attention behind me to a man who stood there twisting a wool scarf in his hands. "Hello, Lissa," he said, and my heart seemed to drop out of my chest. Never mind the handsome man sitting next to me; Gordon Hastings was standing just a few feet away, and he'd just said my name for the first time in…ever. After eight years of actively pretending I didn't exist, my father had suddenly chosen to acknowledge me.

CHAPTER THREE

"I'm going to let you deal with this on your own," Brennon muttered and slipped away before I could complain. Even if he was a little too charming, I would much rather talk to him than the guy on my other side. But he was gone in an instant, leaving me alone.

"What are you doing here?" I snapped. I probably should have been nicer to Gordon, since he *was* my father, but I was neither in the mood nor did I think he deserved it.

He clutched his scarf a little tighter, strangling it with his fingers, and his eyes followed Seth for a moment on the dance floor. "I came to see my son get married," he said. "Though I don't think he knows I'm here."

"Were you actually invited?" Not that I had much personal experience with the guy, but Gordon Hastings wasn't exactly "Father of the Year." Seth had told me plenty of stories about his childhood and how Gordon paid attention only when he was affected by poor behavior. Seth had had to learn early on that his father's approval was not something he would easily get in his lifetime.

Sliding into the chair vacated by Indie, Gordon took a slow breath and muttered, "It was a beautiful ceremony." He looked very much like Seth, with his bright blue eyes and sharp jawline. His hair had gone a bit white since the last time I saw him, though, so it wasn't as sandy blonde as my brother's. It was strange to see him this up close; I'd only ever seen him through a screen. "And Seth didn't tell me I couldn't come, so…"

I wondered what Seth would do as soon as he saw his dad, and I was tempted to hop up and let him know so I could find out. Seth generally kept an even temper, but there were certain things that could get him riled up. His emotionally unavailable father was one of them.

But something else had snagged my brother's attention and made him freeze in the middle of the dance floor. Following his gaze, I took in the balding man who had just stepped through one of the doors—a man who had gone pale when he realized what a terrible idea that was as he locked eyes with Seth.

"Dad?" Catherine said, and a break in the music at just the right moment meant most of the room heard her alarmed question. All eyes turned to the unfolding drama, and the orchestra was suddenly playing to an uninterested crowd. "What are you doing here?"

The man at the door swallowed, looking around the room as if in search of allies. He reminded me a lot of my assistant when he knew he'd made a mistake and had to tell me about it. "Catherine," he said then clamped his jaw shut.

"Answer the question, Milton," Seth said, and his voice was low in his throat. Almost a growl, like a dog giving a warning before he attacked. He was so stiff that he looked like he might snap, and even when Catherine took his hand, he didn't move a muscle.

Milton Davenport was much like my own father in that he was an elite, one of the rich and powerful with more money than they knew what to do with. But unlike pretty much everyone at this wedding, who were the best of the best and looked it, he did not wear his status well. He was a little more on the disheveled side, too thin for a man who probably had a personal chef, and he had far more lines in his face than he should. What little I knew of Catherine's father didn't help his poor image. The guy had actively ignored ransom calls when Catherine was kidnapped by terrorists four years ago, and he still hadn't acknowledged the event despite it being headlining news for months after the fact. Catherine had spent every summer and holiday since then with her cousins here in California, and Seth had kept her despicable father away from her. Until now.

I glanced back at Gordon and frowned. When Seth had been taken by the same men, Gordon had done the exact same thing.

"I have a right to be here," Milton said, and his eyes swept the banquet hall again as the orchestra members stopped playing so they could pay attention to the drama as well. "You can't keep me away from my own daughter, Hastings."

Catherine lunged forward, but Seth caught her arm before she got very far. "Your *daughter?*" she said, and her voice held even more anger than her glare. "Since when have you considered me your daughter? Seth, let go of me."

But Seth held fast. "I can make him leave," he reminded his wife quietly. Considering he was used to charging head first into enemy fire—and probably missed that part of military life—he was keeping a surprisingly cool head and almost smiled at Catherine's attempts to free herself. "I don't want you to ruin your dress, my love. He's not worth it."

"He's just here for the publicity," Catherine snapped. "As always."

When Milton rolled his eyes, the tension in the room shifted a bit. Instead of being completely still, Seth fluidly transitioned into a fighting stance, his hand still on Catherine's arm. Ready to defend if needed.

"You have always been so self-important, silly girl," Milton said with a huff. "Just like your mother."

From what I could tell, everyone within ten feet of the interaction looked as ready to run as Seth looked to attack. They were all smart enough to know that it was a terrible idea to mess with the likes of my brother, particularly when it came to his wife.

"I think it's time for you to go," Seth said carefully. His eyes were on Catherine and the way she suddenly seemed on the verge of tears. I didn't know much about her mother, just that she'd died when Catherine was young.

I held my breath in anticipation. This short conversation felt like it was right on the edge of its breaking point, and I wasn't sure it would end well.

"Go," Catherine whispered. "You don't belong here."

"I am a Davenport," Milton snarled back, and he grabbed Catherine's wrist.

Someone screamed as Seth moved so quickly that I barely saw it. He suddenly had Milton's throat in his hand, though he didn't hold tight enough to do any damage. Yet. "You're done with this family," he said, and he sounded just as calm as ever, even if his voice seemed to have dropped an octave.

Milton, on the other hand, stood as tall as his fear allowed and set his jaw, trying to hold his ground. But I could practically feel his utter terror. Seth was so much bigger than him in every way.

"If I get even a whiff of you trying to ruin this family more than you already have," Seth continued, "you'll find out exactly how far I'll go to protect the people I love. You're not a Davenport anymore, and we're done with you."

"Just leave," Catherine added.

Milton sent one pleading look to his daughter then scurried away through the crowd that parted for him easily. I had a feeling, though, that that wasn't the last Seth's family would see of their black sheep.

Seth's stiffness dissipated the instant Milton was gone, and he pulled his wife into his arms and hugged her tight. At the same moment, some intelligent cellist struck up a tune that his fellow musicians quickly picked up with him, easing the tension of the room by epic proportions.

"In a way, I'm glad he came," Gordon said, almost under his breath. I'd practically forgotten he was even here. "I look like a saint by comparison." Seth had managed to get rid of one father; apparently it was my job to get rid of the other, though I wasn't sure I had the energy after watching that bit of drama go down.

"Why are you here?" I asked again, turning my full attention to the man next to me now that the danger had passed.

He burned a bit red and grabbed a flute of champagne from a passing server. "Obviously I'm here to celebrate my son's happy day," he mumbled.

Sure. Our father was about as attentive as Catherine's, though he lacked the sheer idiocy. "Let me rephrase that," I said. "Why are you here talking to *me*?" He had done his best to avoid this exact thing for long enough that I really couldn't wrap my head around the fact that he was sitting right next to me.

His immediate answer died on his tongue the minute he saw my expression.

"Okay," he said, letting out a huff of air. "I know I haven't been very fair to you."

"Understatement of the century," I replied. "Get to the point." I'd never expected anything from the man who seduced my mom then vanished, and I certainly didn't expect anything now. He was just half of a biological equation. Nothing more.

He downed his champagne then took a deep breath. "I want to try, Lissa." *Ha!* "I know that may be hard to believe, but I want to try being your father before it's too late."

Interesting. "What," I asked coolly, "are you dying or something?" Maybe if he had done this when I was eight, I would have considered it, but I gave up on the idea of having a father twenty years ago. I didn't need one. If he wanted to be in my life, he should have made an effort when Seth first told him about me when I was in college.

Paling a little, Gordon resumed twisting his scarf as he fought to find the words that would best work to his advantage. "I almost lost my son a few years ago," he said quietly.

Yes, when Seth was captured and tortured by someone trying to get to *him.* As the Secretary of Homeland Security, Gordon Hastings was worth a lot.

"I know it's taken me a while to realize it," he said, "but... I don't know what I would have done if I'd lost him. I don't want to lose you either, Lissa."

I was too tired for this. I reached for my glass of champagne and drank it in two gulps. After a quick glance around the room, I realized Brennon had entirely disappeared, which only added to my track record of being perpetually single. It was a bit sad how much I wished he would come back. "You know," I said, "in order to lose me, you need to have had me in the first place. You can't just claim me because you've decided to act like you've had a change of heart."

He stood when I did. "Lissa."

"I'm going home tonight," I told him. "You don't have to pretend to want anything to do with me."

"Lissa, wait."

"Hey, Dad." Seth's voice hadn't fully softened from his encounter with Milton Davenport, so when he spoke just behind me, I jumped a little. "What are you doing here?"

To my surprise, Catherine was next to Seth and stepped forward to pull me into a tight side hug. She hadn't talked to me much today— not that I blamed her for focusing elsewhere on her wedding day—but her smile was just as warm as it always was when she and Seth came to visit me. "We can make him leave if you want us to," she said softly.

"Just say the word," Catherine's cousin Matthew added, appearing nearby. What, did the whole family feel the need to come to my rescue when I had everything handled already?

"I'm fine," I told all of them, Gordon included.

"Answer the question, Dad," Seth pressed.

Gordon swallowed, but he wasn't quite as afraid of his son as the rest of the world, maybe because he'd seen him when he was a scrawny little kid playing rich person lacrosse instead of little league. "I wanted to offer congratulations, son. You made a fine choice."

"You're dang right he did," Catherine said, impressively smug. That comment brought a small smile to my lips, and a second later, I realized she and I were now sisters. And I was perfectly okay with that. It took a special woman to deserve my brother, and Catherine was all of that and more. At least something good had come out of today.

Taking one step closer to our father, Seth held out his hand in a reluctant gesture of truce. Gordon was right, if only a little; compared to Catherine's dad, he wasn't nearly as bad as he could have been. "Thanks," Seth said coldly. "And now you can go. I don't need you pretending you actually care about family. Not tonight."

Gordon barely looked at Seth, even while shaking his hand. He kept his gaze locked on me, and I could almost see his sincerity. *Interesting.* "Don't shut me out, Lissa," he said. "I meant what I said."

"I'll keep that in mind," I replied as he wandered out of the room. I still had no idea why he was even bothering. Outside of dying from some horrible disease, he had no real reason to want to try. It was hard to believe he actually cared, not when there were likely other young people out there just like me whose mothers had fallen under Secretary Hastings's spell. But over my time working for Mikaelson, I'd come to learn how to read men and catch the lies behind their words and gestures. Gordon Hastings was telling the truth, and I was almost curious enough to try to figure out why. Was it really because of what almost happened to Seth?

"Now that both our fathers have thoroughly embarrassed us," Catherine said, pulling my attention back to the loving family beside me. "Can we please have some fun? I didn't get married just to add some drama into my life."

Seth laughed and immediately lifted her into his arms to carry her back to the dance floor, bridal style. "Sure you didn't," he said to her, back to his warm and happy self. I'd rarely seen that side of him before he met Catherine, and it was nice to see him content with life for once. He deserved it.

Matthew touched my arm, and I couldn't help but smile at his concern. "Are you sure you're okay?" he asked, and there was an undercurrent of strength in his voice. From the outside, he didn't look like much, but I had a feeling there was more to Matthew Davenport than most people realized. "We're pretty equipped to deal with difficult parents, if you haven't noticed."

I really didn't know much about Matthew, but I knew Catherine considered her cousin to be one of the best men she knew. I could easily see why just from the expression on his face. He would probably face down a man twice his size if he thought I needed him to. "I really am fine," I told him. "Go dance with Indie."

His eyes lit up, and he hurried off.

Leaving me with an empty feeling in my chest.

Some people were meant to find love, and they thrived on it. Most of the time I just hoped I'd get through the day, knowing I would have to do it on my own for the rest of my life. It wasn't like I'd expected to find love at this wedding, but my one chance at romance tonight had disappeared, and that fact certainly followed the pattern of my life. I wasn't naive enough to think I needed a man to be successful—the utter stupidity of that thought had fueled my motivation through business school—but life could get lonely. As much as I knew I was strong enough to live my own life, I would forever wish I could be lucky enough to find a partner to share it with. To face my battles with, side by side. Just like Seth had.

CHAPTER FOUR

Several drinks and three hours later, I finally managed to convince Catherine's cousin, Lanna, to drive me home. Luckily for me, she and her husband were eager to go pick up their young son from Lanna's parents, and I was just drunk enough that they took pity on me and convinced Seth and Catherine to let me go. They dropped me off at Catherine's building with content smiles and their own personal remedies for curing the hangover I'd be facing in the morning.

Though it hadn't been my plan to stay any longer than I had to, I couldn't stomach the idea of hopping on a plane in my current, unsteady state. I couldn't stomach much of anything, and I had to pause at the base of the stairs until the world stopped spinning. *Oh boy.* I took the stairs slowly—no way was I using the elevator—and made sure I took deep, even breaths. I'd overdone it for sure, but I was also pretty sure it was the only way I made it through that wedding. My father's strange declaration coupled with being surrounded by so many adoring couples was a doozy.

Thank goodness for Catherine's apartment or I would have gotten lost trying to navigate an endless hall of identical doors. At least here, there were only three or four apartments per floor—she certainly liked to live large—so I was almost positive I was at the right door. But where in the world was my clutch?

I may have been drunk, but I could easily picture my little purse sitting on the car seat in Lanna's car, which was long gone. As were my phone and the keys to Catherine's apartment. *Oh good.*

Maybe the door was unlocked? I tried it, wiggling the handle as much as I dared without making too much noise, but of course it didn't budge. Seth Hastings was not the kind of guy who would leave his door unlocked.

"I'm thinking you want 202," said a voice behind me.

I jumped, nearly fell over, and pressed a hand against my chest to keep my heart from beating out of it. "Brennon," I gasped. At least, I thought that was his name. The man who didn't believe in love. I'd barely given him a thought after the rest of the drama. "Did you follow me?" That was concerning, and I wondered how hard it would be to get a hold of Matthew. I certainly wasn't going to call Seth to come save me, not on his wedding night. Besides, it wasn't like I had my phone, anyway.

"I'm surprised you can remember," Brennon replied with a chuckle. "Unless you're confusing me with the other me."

"Ha," I grumbled, though he wasn't wrong. Exhaustion and alcohol made it hard to combine both of him into one single image. Oh man, how much did I drink?

He put his hand on my shoulder, and surprisingly that helped keep me steady enough that I could see him more clearly. "For your information," he said, "no. I did not follow you. I actually live here." He held up his keys, and I squinted to see the name of the building on his little shiny keychain.

"Oh," I said. "Right. That's how you know Catherine." Would it be rude if I just stopped talking to him and settled down on the floor? I just wanted to go to bed. "For someone who doesn't believe in love," I mumbled, "you spent a lot of time at your neighbor's wedding."

His smile really was breathtaking. "Just because I'm a bit of a cynic doesn't mean I can't have some fun," he said.

"Fun." I blew air through my lips then decided I had best sit down before I fell over. It wasn't easy in the dress Catherine had put me in, but I managed to get myself against the wall with a little effort.

To my surprise, Brennon sat next to me, close enough that I was acutely aware of his cologne wafting over to me but far enough that we weren't touching. "I probably had more fun than you, unfortunately," he said gently. "I'm sorry your father showed up and made things weird for you."

It wasn't that he made things weird. He made me confused. It had been so long since I wanted his recognition that I wasn't sure what to do with it now that I had it. "You can't choose your family," I mumbled, squinting a bit as I tried to keep Brennon's face in focus.

He smiled again, probably because I could barely get the words out. "No, you can't," he agreed. He seriously smelled amazing. I hadn't been close enough to notice at the wedding, but he smelled like timber wolves and pine. "Timber wolves?" he asked with a laugh.

Oh, sweet mercy. "I said that out loud," I whispered, absolutely mortified. I rarely drank, mostly because it tended to open up my mouth when I wanted to keep it shut. Life was easier when I had full control over myself.

"Beautiful *and* poetic," Brennon said. He was quiet after that, the silence stretching out between us until I couldn't handle it anymore.

"So what's your story, Brennon Ashworth?" I asked, bumping his shoulder with mine. I hoped his response would answer a completely unrelated question: *Why would you be interested in me?*

He smiled, his pearly whites glittering in the fluorescent glow of the hall light as he looked up at the ceiling. "My story's pretty boring," he said. "Grew up here. Went to Stanford. Got a job and have been there ever since."

"You're right," I said, "that's pretty boring." I had to wonder if whatever he was leaving out was worth digging for, but I so did not have the energy—or the sobriety—to find out.

Laughing, he held his hand palm up on his leg and raised an eyebrow. Tempting me. "What about you?" he said when I took that hand and pulled it into my lap so I could play with his fingers. "What about your story? Please tell me it's more interesting than mine."

I shrugged. "What do you want to know?" I said. But that was dangerous, so I quickly added, "And I reserve the right to refuse to answer, so choose your questions carefully."

"Do I get a limit?"

Limit. Yeah, that was probably smart. "Three," I said. "And you can't ask for more questions. That's cheating."

He put on a thoughtful face and rubbed my thumb with his as he gazed down at our hands. "Only three, huh? Hmm. Okay, first, are you from California, or somewhere else?"

That was an easy enough question to answer. "I grew up in Vermont," I said. "I currently live in Boston."

"That's a long way to come for a wedding."

He wasn't wrong. Sighing, I dropped my head against the wall and tried not to think too hard about what was waiting for me back on the East Coast. "Well," I said, "I couldn't exactly miss my brother's wedding."

"I was under the impression you would not be attending," Brennon countered. "Catherine was all sorts of upset about it. Complained constantly. I started having to avoid her in the hallway just so I wouldn't have to hear another word about how the wedding was ruined because Seth's sister didn't approve and thought green was a terrible color for the bridesmaids and—"

"You can shut up now," I said and gave him a glare. I so hoped he was kidding and that Catherine hadn't actually thought that about me. I was a terrible sister in a lot of ways, but there was no one better for my brother than her. If I had thought not attending would have made Catherine think I didn't like her, I never would have let myself forget the wedding.

I hoped.

"You're wrong, you know," Brennon said.

"About what?"

"Green is a great color."

"I never said—shut up," I growled and threw his hand back over to his own lap. I instantly missed his warm fingers and the distraction they had been. Now I could hardly concentrate on anything but the headache pounding in my skull.

Laughing yet again, Brennon simply scooted closer and leaned his head against mine. He seriously smelled *so good*. "Are you ready for my second question?" he asked.

"If I have to be. Though technically that *was* a question."

"Why would you come all this way just to be miserable?"

I sat up so I could look at him then promptly pressed a hand to my temple as the world swayed a bit around me. "You think I'm miserable?" He didn't have to answer that question, since I was pretty sure I hadn't really been trying to hide it. "Right," I muttered. "Well, it's not like I'm not happy for Seth and Catherine. The wedding was great."

"But?"

"But I just lost my job. I mean I quit my job." There was a difference. "So I'm a little stressed at the moment." And I didn't want to be talking about this, particularly with a man who clearly had his life together. His apartment building alone was a testament to that. "I should get some sleep," I said with a sigh. There was little point in dragging this out. "It was good to meet you, Brennon."

"I still have one more question," he replied.

I was regretting giving him three, and I vowed to never get tipsy when I might be in the company of men like Brennon Ashworth. Men who were too charming for their own good. There was no telling what my tongue might say. "I still might not answer," I reminded him.

But he simply smiled and hopped up to his feet, offering his hand. "Do you trust me enough to sleep on my couch tonight?" he said. "It might be a little better than a hallway floor."

All of my single gal sensibilities screamed at me, telling me that accepting an invitation into a strange man's apartment was a terrible idea. But this was Catherine's neighbor. She would have warned me if she lived next to a creep, right? Besides, he was right. If I spent all night in this hallway, it would only be even harder to get myself back on track once morning hit. I wasn't helpless, and if Brennon tried anything...

He must have seen something in my expression, because he smiled and crouched back down so he was at eye level with me. "I promise I'm not the kind of guy to try something skeezy," he said gently. "In fact, I don't think I've ever used the word skeezy before. But if it makes you feel any better, I am very away that you're Seth Hastings's sister. I'm smart enough to know when I'm outmatched, and I have no intention of seeing if you live up to your name."

He made a good point. If Seth had any reason to think I'd been poorly treated, Brennon would be lucky to escape with his life. But it wasn't that thought that made me take his hand and let him pull me up to my feet. It was the idea that a man could think I was capable on my own. I had almost stopped believing such a thing was possible.

I woke with a start and immediately regretted all my life choices.

I was never going to drink again. It wasn't worth the hammer in my head and the churning in my stomach. Or maybe that was the three pieces of cheesecake. Oh man, I felt awful. It had been so long since I slept anywhere but on my outrageously priced mattress that I'd forgotten how stiff I could get when sleeping on something like a couch, and my entire spine felt like it had melded into a single piece.

Wait. Couch. Sleep.

I sat straight up as my heart burst into double-time. What had I done? Oh man, I was way too drunk to let a man lead me into his apartment, no matter how trustworthy he seemed, and while I had very little memory of the night before, I could recall getting awfully snuggly with a guy I didn't even know. How stupid could I be? But a quick investigation, along with some foggy memories of Brennon pulling a blanket over me then disappearing, told me I was fine. Nothing had happened. I was stupid, but I was fine.

I might as well have been wearing a sign around my neck that said, "Lissa Montgomery: Maker of Bad Decisions since Last Week." First quitting my job, and now this. I was on a roll. And I was usually so responsible…

"Brennon is a lot of things," someone said suddenly, and I gasped and turned to the stranger sitting at a kitchen table. A bowl of cereal sat in front of him, and pain-inducing sunshine from the window behind him threw him into silhouette. "But, to my never-ending disappointment, he is not a pig. So he's got that going for him."

That wasn't Brennon. While I was thinking about it, where *was* Brennon? Had he just abandoned me the moment I passed out?

Either I asked the question out loud or he could read my thoughts, because the Cereal Guy finished loudly chewing and said, "Like any respectable stockbroker, my idiotic roommate went to work on a Sunday instead of making breakfast for the pretty girl he brought home from a wedding."

Roommate. Seriously? I'd naturally assumed, given the location of his apartment and his proximity to the likes of Catherine Davenport, that Brennon wasn't exactly wanting for money. His Armani suit may have helped lead to that conclusion, so why on earth would he need a roommate? Maybe the guy was lonely. After all, he didn't believe in love.

But first things first. "He didn't bring me home," I mumbled, trying to untangle myself from the blanket over me. Only then did I remember I was wearing someone else's clothes, since Brennon had rightfully guessed I was less than enthused about remaining in my too-tight dress. Brennon's shirt smelled just like him, and I took a deep breath with my nose in the collar. "I live across the hall," I added, remembering that I wasn't sitting here alone. I reached for my dress, where it rested on the back of the couch, and tried to shake myself awake.

Cereal Guy cleared his throat then dumped some more cereal into his bowl, each little piece bouncing around inside my skull as it hit the bowl. "Not that I claim to know Catherine Davenport well," he said, "but I'm pretty sure you're not her."

Well duh. Catherine was flawless, way too intelligent to accept an invitation like I had. She probably didn't even drink anymore. "She's my..." Wow, I really needed some coffee or water or a new head altogether. What was that word? "She's my new sister-in-law. I'm staying at her place until I head back to Boston."

Now where did I put my shoes?

Cereal was almost silent as he watched me dig around the blankets in search of the heels that had given me good and proper blisters, the crunch of his chewing the only sound he made. But when I kicked my toe into the coffee table and shouted a curse, he snorted half a laugh.

"Who even are you?" I demanded as I curled my toes against the pain. One shoe poked out from under the table, though, and I was pretty sure the other had to be nearby.

"Steve," he said lightly. "Bren's my best friend, even if he can be an idiot."

I had to crawl beneath the table to reach and probably looked like an idiot myself with my rear end sticking up behind me in pants that were not mine. "What's that supposed to mean?" I grunted.

"He's out there earning a living and missing the fun here at home."

Banging my head on the table above me, I bit back another curse but only because I needed that anger to give this Steve a decent glare. "I'm glad you're entertained," I said.

"Oh, I definitely am. I don't even remember the last time I had this much fun."

I wished I could see his face so I could see if it matched his cocky, manly voice, but the sun was way too bright behind him. Looking at him too closely would probably kill me with the added headache it would bring. "Do you always laugh at helpless women?" I asked.

"Just the ones who pretend they're not," he said lightly. "Though I'm not sure I would call you helpless."

"What would you call me then?"

"Desperate."

"Excuse me?"

He laughed for real, though it sounded off. Almost wrong. Like he'd forgotten how to do it properly. "Don't get me wrong," he said. "I'm sure you're very smart and capable. But you could do so much better than Brennon Ashworth." If he wasn't struggling to hold back his laughter, I'd almost think he was serious. And for some reason that made me smile. Only a true best friend would say something like that, and it was clear he thought very highly of Brennon.

"Well thanks for the warning," I said, finally locating my other shoe and moving to the door so I could figure out how to get my clutch from Lanna, since I had no idea where she lived or how to get in touch with her. "I'll be sure to tell him you said so." I had no intention of seeing Brennon again, though, since my flight was later that day. He would just have to be a pleasant and somewhat alarming memory. Proof that I wasn't a lost cause but should probably work on my self-control before I got myself into trouble.

"Happy to oblige," Steve replied, and when I glanced back, I caught a glimpse of a smile in the sunlight.

So maybe Brennon wasn't what I thought he was. He hadn't taken advantage of me last night, and his best friend obviously thought well of him. And while he wasn't exactly original with his pickup lines and advances, at least he was honest. And sympathetic. It was too bad I wasn't staying longer, or I might actually consider seeing if maybe he—

I stopped just as I reached for the doorknob and stared at my clutch, which sat on a little shelf that hung right next to the door. With it was a note:

> *I called Lanna Munroe last night after you fell asleep so someone would know where you were, and she brought your things over this morning. While I enjoyed our little hallway chat, I'd love the chance to get to know you when you're sober. Meet me for brunch?*
> *— Bren*

Whoa. Never mind the dude left me a handwritten note—and had impeccably neat handwriting—but I couldn't remember the last time a man had actually *wanted* to meet sober me after meeting the much less uptight drunk me. Then there was the fact that he had apparently called Catherine's cousin, and not just to earn himself some points, since I was already fast asleep at that point. That was above and beyond what any decent human would do. Was Brennon Ashworth even real?

My head hurt, my back ached, and I had a flight in a few hours, but as I stood there looking at the time and place he suggested and thinking about how much I wanted to see his ridiculously handsome smile again, I was quickly running out of reasons why I shouldn't spend my last few hours in California with him. What would I do otherwise? Flip through TV channels and sip a sports drink until my cab arrived to bring me back to my big fat load of nothing in Boston.

Coffee and quiche with an attractive guy sounded a whole lot better.

CHAPTER FIVE

"You came!" Brennon's smile hit me hard, nearly tripping me as I stepped onto the sidewalk outside the cafe. Dang, he'd managed to look even more attractive, which I didn't think was possible. A tailored suit was generally the best attire for looking good, and yet Brennon Ashworth managed to outdo himself with a simple button-up shirt and dark jeans. It made him look a little more human.

"You sound surprised," I said. Goodness, he even pulled out my chair for me.

"I hope you won't get too cold sitting outside," he continued without acknowledging my comment. "I like to get fresh air when I can, and that isn't often."

I glanced down at the sweater I'd chosen and couldn't help but grin. "Yeah, I grew up in Vermont, remember?" I said. "I'll be fine." In fact, I was almost regretting not wearing a shirt and jacket so I could take the jacket off once the sun got higher and get some color. No wonder Seth liked living out here, where even in December the air was pretty warm. I was used to snow and lots of it.

Brennon's smile grew wider. "Good," he said. "Coffee?"

"You read my mind." For a man who didn't believe in love, he certainly knew how to act on a date. Assuming this was a date. I honestly wasn't sure, not that it really mattered.

"I hope you slept okay," he said, giving me an unusual amount of eye contact. I couldn't decide if it was refreshing or unnerving, but I wasn't about to stop him from doing it. For once, a man seemed to want to know what was going through my head. "I thought about letting you use my bed and taking the couch myself," he continued, "but I didn't want to move you. You looked so…peaceful."

That twitch of his lips said otherwise. "How bad was I?" I asked. "I snored, didn't I?"

Still fighting his smile, he shrugged a little and pretended to be fascinated by the menu in front of him. "Drooled," he coughed.

I should have been mortified. And while yes, my face felt like it was on fire, it wasn't because I was embarrassed. It was because Brennon lifted his eyes to meet mine and somehow managed to convey with a single look that he had absolutely no problem with the way I had acted last night. In fact, I suspected he almost found it endearing.

Seriously, how was he real?

"That's just my way of marking my territory," I replied, and my face burned again. Definitely shouldn't have said that.

But he laughed loud enough that a couple of people turned to see what was so amusing, and I found myself smiling along with him. "Lissa Montgomery," he said, shaking his head. Apparently, he didn't mind my inability to keep my thoughts to myself. "You are nothing like I expected, and I'm liking you more and more as the time goes by. Where have you been hiding all this time?"

Way too far away, apparently.

"So wait," Brennon said, a piece of avocado stuck to the end of his fork as he pointed it at me. "You have a dual degree in economics and business from *Yale*, and you were never made partner? You've got to be kidding."

Shrugging, I fought back memories of the faces of triumph I had to pass with my box of belongings as I left Mikaelson and Hewitt a few days ago. "That's how it goes for a woman," I said and fought against a sigh. I wasn't trying to be self-deprecating or even fishing for pity. It was fact, simple as that.

Brennon shook his head and set his fork on his plate before he threw food everywhere. "Maybe on the East Coast," he said, "but not here. Our VP is a woman, and she's, well, honestly she's more terrifying than any of the men I work with."

Exactly. "Because she has to be," I replied. "If she was any more feminine, any softer, she probably couldn't have gotten that far." This was not where I wanted our conversation to turn, and I frantically tried to find a way to bring our discussion back to music where it had been an hour earlier. This shift to my job—or lack of—was not where I'd wanted the focus to end up.

"Maybe," he admitted, "but maybe not. I can see why you left. If they weren't smart enough to realize you could have saved some of those companies millions of dollars, they don't deserve you. You could come work with me!"

Whoa now. I laughed to cover the sheer terror that filled me at his comment. "I'm going back to Boston in three hours, Bren." When had I started calling him Bren?

"You don't have to," he argued, his gaze so intense that I couldn't look away even though I had a delightful bite of toast left on my plate that I wanted to devour. There was nothing in the world quite like San Franciscan sourdough. "It's not like you have a job to go back to."

Technically that was true, but—

"Besides, I kind of like sitting across from you and watching you try not to look at that last bit of food. You can eat it, you know."

I had to be dreaming. No man could be this perfect, and yet he sat there clear as day, holding back a breathtaking grin and easily breaking through my excuses. If I wasn't careful, this self-proclaimed love cynic was going to uproot my entire existence, and I wasn't totally sure that was a bad thing. There was just one thing…

"I don't want to work in finance," I said, and it felt like a weight had just lifted from my shoulders. I hadn't even considered the idea until just that moment, but the epiphany was absolutely liberating. Being a financial analyst was still fighting for a place in a man's world, and until that changed, I was tired of being asked to get coffee and getting interrupted every other sentence. Helping rich corporations get richer wasn't fulfilling. It never had been. "I don't want to be that kind of woman."

Brennon's smile softened, warmer than ever. "What kind of woman do you want to be?" he asked.

I took a deep breath. "I have no idea. Someone who helps people, not companies. Someone who can actually make a difference in someone else's life. Whatever that means."

"Well." He reached out, sliding his fingers between mine and practically looking into my soul as we sat there. What did he see? "What if…" He actually looked a little nervous. "What if you stay a little longer, and I can help you figure that out? I'd love to go on a third date, if you're willing."

Adorable. "Sitting in a hallway when I'm completely drunk does not count as a date," I said, though I smiled at him and held onto his hand a little tighter. This was a terrible idea.

"Fine," he said. "A second date, then. I really am glad you came this morning."

I grinned. "I happen to like brunch."

"Brunch," he replied, shaking his head. "You're really something, Lissa Montgomery." But then his face fell, and he pulled his phone from his pocket and glanced at the screen. "Sorry," he muttered before lifting it to his ear. "Steve?"

I took a couple of deep breaths while he listened to his roommate, trying to convince myself that I was not allowed to let myself get in too deep with this specimen in front of me. No matter how charming he was, no matter how sincere he seemed, this was still a guy who flat-out admitted he didn't believe in love, which begged the question of where he thought this thing would go if I stayed. If I let myself think there was even a possibility with the guy, I would end up getting hurt, just like I always did. No, better to keep a safe distance if I could.

"Is he okay?" Brennon asked into his phone, his voice strained. That didn't sound good. "I understand. Thank you. Yeah, I'll be there as soon as I can." When he hung up, he was pale, almost shaking as he sat there, and my stomach twisted in my gut.

"Brennon?"

He blinked, and I was surprised to see tears in his eyes. "That was, um, the hospital near my condo," he said. "My roommate, Steve, was hit by a car."

Horrified, I put a hand to my mouth. "Is he okay?" I asked, speaking his own question back at him.

Slowly pulling his hand away from mine, Brennon shrugged. The suave and carefree man was gone, replaced by one who clearly didn't know how he was supposed to act anymore. "I think so," he mumbled. "I don't know. They said he's pretty banged up. Sorry, but I need..." Swallowing, he got to his feet and stood there looking completely lost. "I have to go. I'm sorry."

He took one step before I grabbed his arm and stopped him. "Let me come with you," I said. "Please. You sound like you need a friend."

He stood there and stared at me for a long several seconds, a range of emotions crossing his face. Then he slipped his hand into mine and gave it a squeeze. "Thank you," he whispered then led the way to his car.

Fortunately, Brennon wasn't so shaken that he couldn't drive, considering I had no idea how to navigate this city. He kept a tight hold on my hand as he drove, and I liked to think I was actually doing him some good. He seemed calmer with me next to him, and I hated thinking how anxious he might be without someone with him. And, though it made me feel a little terrible, I was infinitely more attracted to him knowing he was so worried about his friend. Most of the guys I had dated in the past wouldn't have been nearly this concerned.

Besides, it was kind of nice to see something break through his easy confidence.

"So what happened?" I asked, trying to fill the silence.

He glanced at me. "They said he was crossing the street when the light was green."

"Didn't he notice the 'do not walk' sign?"

"Well obviously he couldn't." Something about that sounded odd.

"Why is that obvious?"

"Because he's…" He paused and glanced at me again, as if only just realizing what he'd started to say. "Blind," he finished quietly.

My eyes went wide. "He's what now?"

"Blind. Mostly."

That didn't make any sense. Sure, I didn't see his face that morning, but the guy was talking to me like normal, even looking at me. Or maybe it was just in my direction. Oh man, how had I not noticed something like that? Just how drunk *was* I? "Blind," I repeated.

"Yeah. He doesn't usually leave the house, so I don't worry about him too much." *I* would worry about someone never leaving the house, but Brennon kept talking: "What was he doing crossing a street on his own?"

I assumed that question was rhetorical. "I'm sure he's fine," I said. "They would have told you if he wasn't."

"Probably," he replied, though he didn't seem convinced.

We found a parking spot close to the entrance of the hospital, and I uncharacteristically thanked my long legs for helping me keep up with his quick strides as we rushed inside. I wasn't sure he would have slowed down to wait for me if I wasn't so tall. Brennon was on a mission, and I followed with a million thoughts running through my head, particularly about how worried he was. He may not have been big into the concept of love, but he was proving his own belief wrong as he rushed to the aid of his friend.

"Steven Evans," Brennon said when we reached the counter, a little breathless and once again shaking. I slipped my arm around his waist to hold him steady, and he responded by sliding his own across my shoulders. "I'm his emergency contact, and they told me he was brought in about an hour ago."

The nurse at the front desk nodded and turned to his computer, scrolling for a second before he looked back up at us. "He's still in the ER," he said. "Straight down the hall to your right."

"Thank you," Brennon replied, but the words barely made a sound. Now *I* was starting to get worried.

We walked almost as quickly as we had outside, and I tried to think of something to say to help Brennon calm down a bit before we reached the emergency room. I hadn't spent a ton of time in hospitals, but I meant what I said. If something was seriously wrong, they would have told him over the phone. Steve was probably fine, maybe just a little bruised, and—

Brennon suddenly slipped out of my hold and sprinted the last several yards, pushing past a resident who tried to grab him before he got to the curtained beds ahead. He must have recognized his friend from a distance, because he went straight for one of the beds on the left and threw the curtains aside.

"What do you think you were doing?" he practically shouted at the man lying there.

I hurried forward and grabbed his arm, ready to tell him to keep his voice down, but I froze the moment I saw Steve. He looked terrible. Blood caked in his curly brown hair and on the side of his head where a few Steri-Strips held a gash in his yellowy skin together. His left arm rested bound against his chest, a bag of ice sat strapped to his left knee, and if he hadn't been lying there with his dark eyes open, I might have wondered if he was even breathing because he was so still. But his mouth twisted in an annoyed grimace, his eyebrows pulled low, and his tongue worked the inside of his mouth as he searched for a response to Brennon's angry question.

"I told them not to call you," he finally mumbled, clearly not as surprised by the outburst as I was. "We were out of bread."

Brennon turned almost as red as Steve was pale. "I know," he growled, and he clenched his hands into fists at his side. "I was going to get some on my way home."

"I'm perfectly capable of walking to the store."

"Obviously not."

"Brennon," I said, taking his arm. He was making things worse.

Steve turned his head a little, his eyes unfocused. "The sister-in-law?" he asked, more curious than I expected him to be. He recognized my voice just from that one word? "Why are you here?"

Brennon groaned a little and pulled away from my touch so he could run both hands down his face. "She's here because you interrupted our date."

"Oh."

"Don't you 'oh' me, you son of a—"

"Brennon!" I said loudly and grabbed his hand, pulling him several feet away from the bed. "Don't you think you're being a little harsh?"

He immediately shook his head, eyes locked on the man in the bed. "Absolutely not. He nearly got himself killed." It was going to take a lot to talk him down, but I knew I had to do it before the anxious interns nearby decided we needed to leave altogether. A part of me wondered if that was a better option than sticking around when Brennon was this riled up. He needed to calm down.

I pressed my palm to his cheek, and his eyes jumped to me in surprise. "Hey," I said gently. "Just be glad he's okay."

For a few long seconds, I worried he would stay angry and keep yelling at his roommate until hospital security arrived to escort us out. But then he sighed and wrapped his fingers around mine, pulling my hand from his jaw and to his lips. "Lissa Montgomery," he whispered, sending heat blazing into my cheeks.

Taking one deep breath, he intertwined our fingers then slowly moved back to the bed. "Sorry," he mumbled. "How're you feeling?"

Though Steve didn't look at anything in particular—How much could he actually see, anyway?—I could almost feel his focus on me. I scooted a little closer to Brennon.

"Drugged," he grunted and rolled his eyes.

Brennon matched the expression. "This is why I told you to get a dog," he said.

"I don't need a dog," Steve replied.

"What he needs is constant supervision for the next week," a deep voice threw in behind us.

Brennon and I both turned, stepping aside to let the ER physician check Steve's vitals. "Supervision?" Brennon asked when the doctor didn't offer up more explanation.

Clipboard in hand, the physician nodded and studied the notes written on the page. "Your friend is lucky to be alive," he said. Steve rolled his eyes again. "He has a few bruised ribs, and that knee is going to give him some trouble for the next few days. But I'm worried about that head injury, given his history, and I can't force him to stay here under observation, as much as I'd like to."

Was it just me, or was Brennon suddenly paler than Steve? "Worried," he repeated.

The doctor scribbled something then looked right at us. "There's no sign of a concussion, but we can't rule out the possibility considering his condition. He shouldn't be left alone for more than a couple of hours, not until we're sure he's avoided anything more serious than surface injuries."

"What about an MRI?" Brennon asked. "CT scan?"

This time it was the doctor who rolled his eyes. "He won't let us, which is why I recommend supervision."

"I'm fine," Steve tried, but neither Brennon nor the doctor paid him any attention.

"I can do that," Brennon assured him, though his fingers tightened a little around mine. "I can keep an eye on him." *Could* he do that?

"Here are some prescriptions for the pain," the doctor continued as he handed Brennon a little slip of paper, "and I'll grab a nurse to help you get him ready to go. He's pretty eager."

Brennon glanced down at the paper then shook the doctor's hand. "Thanks, Dave," he said. He was on a first-name basis with the doc?

Steve sat up the moment *Dave* was gone, pulling the heart monitor sensor from his finger and swinging his legs over the side of the bed. "Shall we?" he asked and stood.

"Whoa!" Brennon replied and pushed his friend back onto the bed before he could take a step. "Where do you think you're going?"

"Home."

"Not until I know everything you need."

"I told you I'm fine."

"Lissa, help me."

I blinked as both of them looked right at me. More or less on Steve's part. Did Brennon really think I could say anything that would change

Steve's mind about getting out of the hospital as soon as possible? I barely knew either of these men, and I wasn't exactly comfortable with the request. But I had to say something, so I said the first thing that came to mind: "He does have a little more color than before, Brennon. Maybe he really is okay."

A smile almost cracked the scowl on Steve's face, and his uninjured eyebrow lifted just a touch as his eyes focused harder on the space just in front of me. "See?" he said quietly. "Like I said."

Brennon was about to argue when a nurse came between the pair of them with a determined smile that said she'd heard every word of the argument. "Okie doke," she said and began unstrapping the ice from Steve's knee. "Best to keep weight off that leg as much as possible until the swelling goes down, and don't take any ibuprofen for at least two days or you'll make your ribs worse." She handed a piece of paper to Brennon that looked like it contained the same instructions she was saying out loud. "Ice packs are good—here's one in case you don't have one—and make sure you breathe and cough normally unless you want to cause pneumonia. Try to take a few deep breaths every—"

"I got it," Steve grunted, practically leaping from the bed as soon as his leg was free. "I've been through this before."

I didn't like the sound of that. How many times had the guy been hit by cars?

"Anything else?" Brennon asked the nurse as Steve started limping away.

She shook her head, more amused than worried as she watched him hobble for the door. "Try to survive him. I wasn't here the last couple of times, but I've heard the stories. He really does live up to the legend."

Stuffing the instructions and the prescription into his pocket, Brennon took a long, deep breath and shut his eyes as he let it out slowly. I had so many questions, but I figured now was not the best time to ask him. He was stressed enough as it was. "Sometimes…" he muttered to himself without finishing the thought, and then together we followed Steve out to the parking lot.

CHAPTER SIX

By the time we got back to Brennon's apartment after stopping at the pharmacy, Steve had taken to muttering expletives under his breath and complaining that Brennon was driving too slowly. He led the way up the stairs, using his hand on the wall as a guide, and was in the apartment before we had even hit the landing of the second floor. He was kind enough to leave the door open for us, at least, but I could feel the tension between the two men even without fully understanding it.

Brennon paused out in the hall and pulled me in for a tight hug when I stopped beside him. "Thank you," he whispered into my ear, sending a shiver through me. "I don't know what I would have done without you there."

I'd do it again if it meant I got to stand here in his arms like this. I hadn't thought anything remarkable about Brennon last night at the wedding outside of his surface-level charms, but I was quickly realizing there was a lot more to this man than I could learn in a couple of days. And oddly enough, I found myself wanting to learn as much as I could. "I was happy to help," I said, wrapping my arms around his waist and pulling myself in tighter. I couldn't keep myself from smiling when his heartbeat kicked up a notch. "And maybe I can keep helping."

He pulled away enough to look at me, confusion and hope in his stunning blue eyes. "What do you mean? Are you going to stay in California? What about your flight?"

Laughing, I shook my head. "My flight left an hour ago. And before you start apologizing, since I have a feeling it's on the tip of your tongue, I cancelled it on our way to the hospital. Seth paid for it, anyway, and he can afford me missing it." In fact, I was pretty sure my brother would be thrilled that I was taking some time off like this, even if he didn't get to spend it with me. He was always saying I worked too hard.

Brennon looked a little too excited as he stared at me. "You're staying?" he repeated, as if he couldn't imagine anything better.

"I'm staying," I replied. "And I'll stay with Steve."

He didn't understand at first, his eyebrows pulling together as he glanced through the open door into his apartment. But then it clicked, and his eyes went wide. "You don't have to do that," he said hesitantly. Hoping I would argue.

"I know I don't *have* to," I replied with a smile, "but I want to. You obviously have work to do and can't be here twenty-four seven, and I've got nothing on my plate and a whole lot of spare time to fill. It only makes sense."

"That would be incredible. At least for now. I have to go back to the office for a couple of hours, but…" He waited half a second, during which his eyes flicked down to my mouth and made me grin, and then he bent down and pressed his lips to mine, giving me a stomach-clenching kiss that made heat spread from my lips to my toes. *Wow.* Fingers in my hair, he touched his forehead to mine and took a shaky breath. "Where did you come from?" he whispered, as if I were sent by some higher power.

So much for keeping my distance. "Boston," I replied and snatched the bag of medicines from his hand, backing into the apartment and leaving him grinning back at me. "I thought I told you that."

As soon as I shut the door, I felt a pair of eyes on me and turned to see Steve standing near the fridge with an ice pack pressed against his rib cage. Though I doubted he could see me, it was a little unnerving how easily he found me against the backdrop of an exposed brick wall almost the same color as my sweater. "Boston?" he asked.

Oh goodness, how much had he heard from the hallway? Hopefully just that. "Yeah," I said. "You ever been?" That was probably a terrible question to ask a man who apparently rarely ventured outside his own front door, and I winced.

But Steve shrugged and muttered, "Couple times," as he limped over to the couch and dropped onto it with a grunt. "Autumn is…" He swallowed, frowning a little. "*Was* my favorite time to go."

Now what was I supposed to say to that? "Did you go there for work, or…?"

"For fun," he said, adjusting his ice pack. Then he was silent.

If this was how the next little while was going to go, I was going to have to rethink my offer to stay. I didn't crave attention from friends and family like Catherine sometimes did, but I wasn't exactly a hermit. At least, I hadn't been before I put in twelve hours a day at Mikaelson and Hewitt. I much preferred having someone to talk to, or at least something to do. And while my usual go-to when I needed to busy myself was cleaning, a quick glance around the spacious apartment told me Brennon was assuredly cleaner than I was.

Check mark in the 'pro' column.

Setting the bag of prescriptions on the granite island in the kitchen portion of the large room, I folded my arms and steeled myself for forcing Steve into at least having a little conversation. It would probably be good for him if he really did spend most of his time alone in the apartment like I suspected. "Do you need some lunch?" I asked, trying to keep my voice light. "I can—"

"I'm not broken," he snapped back. "I've been taking care of myself my whole life, and I don't need Brennon's latest toy treating me like a toddler." And then he grabbed a pair of earbuds and stuffed them into his ears, closing his eyes and shutting off the rest of the world.

I glared at him. "Jerk," I muttered.

Now what was I supposed to do?

Catherine's apartment across the hall was huge, but it felt more like a hotel suite with the way each room had its own closed off space. It was cozy and comfortable, and it fit her personality well. Brennon's was similar in size but felt so much bigger with the way the main room flowed seamlessly into the kitchen and entryway, one giant rectangle with a wall full of windows. The kitchen alone, a decent size with plenty of counter space and top-of-the-line appliances, put my Boston place to shame, though I'd already packed up most of my stuff into boxes in preparation of leaving it behind for good. Brennon knew how to decorate, too, keeping things chic and simple while still maintaining a sense of masculinity about the place. He had several dozen books that varied in subjects and topics, a wall full of movies to view on his enormous TV, and I spied a jacuzzi on the little balcony outside. I walked the length of the room in giddy awe until I reached the hallway that led to the bedrooms.

Curiosity got the better of me, and I poked my head through the open door on the left, just beyond the bathroom, excited to realize Brennon kept his room just as neat and orderly as the rest of the apartment. Simple navy sheets and comforter stretched across his king size bed, and more books filled a shelf by the window, many of them books I'd been wanting to read but had never gotten my hands on a copy. Only modern art hung on the walls, giving the space a calm, organized feeling that seemed to fit Brennon well. And the room smelled like him. I couldn't help but open up his closet and take in his fashionable wardrobe, every piece with a lingering scent of timber wolves—*kill me*—and pine.

I paused at a picture in a silver frame on the table beside his bed, and my chest seized up a little. A slightly younger Brennon smiled wide in the photo and looked enormously happy in his tux. The girl who latched onto his arm, with flattering black gown and perfect, tight golden curls, looked even more so as she laughed from the frame. As I stood there trying to discern any features that could make her a sister or a cousin or anything that wasn't a girlfriend or worse, Steve's last words rang in my ears.

I don't need Brennon's latest toy treating me like a toddler.

Just how often did the man's charms work on women like me?

"Don't be an idiot," I mumbled out loud, sitting on his bed and looking anywhere but the photo that was several years old, at least. "Why should I care if he dates other people? It's not like we're officially a couple, and I barely know him. I have no intentions of falling in love—ha!—and neither does he, so it doesn't matter. I'll just enjoy it while it lasts then head back to Boston where I belong." And stop talking to myself before Steve decided I was crazy, since I would guess his hearing was definitely better than his eyesight.

Suddenly in a bad mood and exceptionally tired from a long couple of days, I slid beneath the covers and promptly fell asleep in the bed of a man who was probably a terrible idea.

At first, I wasn't sure what woke me, though I recalled something crashing in my dream. Maybe I hadn't heard anything at all. But then a rough curse carried down the hallway and made me sit up. Steve?

Rubbing sleep from my eyes and wondering what time it was, I stumbled down the hall into the bright lights of the front room. Upon first glance, I saw nothing, but then Steve appeared from behind the counter with what looked like a handful of sopping noodles in his cupped hands. What in the...? Slowly, trying to decide how best to announce my presence as he ducked down again and brought up another handful of wet cavatappi to dump into the sink, I made my way around the counter and discovered an entire pot of soup spilled across the floor and a lit burner currently heating nothing but air.

I knew I shouldn't laugh, and I really tried not to, but a snicker escaped me anyway.

Steve froze halfway through his next scoop of noodles and shut his eyes tight. "Don't say it," he begged.

I grinned. "Want me to make you some food?" I offered again. "Or are you planning on licking that up off the floor?" Given what little I knew about the guy, it was so not my place to find anything about this funny, but I couldn't help it, especially when his ears burned red beneath his curly hair but he tried so hard to look unaffected. If he had been nicer to me earlier, it would have been a lot easier to feel bad for him.

"Fine," he grumbled after a few seconds then grabbed a towel where it hung by the stove and began sopping up the broth at his feet.

He'd washed his face, I realized as I watched him. Most of the blood was gone, leaving just the strips of adhesive over the gash above his eyebrow. Now that he wasn't strapped to a hospital bed beneath fluorescent lights, I wasn't sure what to make of him. If not for his too-long hair and unkempt beard, he might have been a handsome sort of guy, though his overlarge sweatshirt and worn jeans didn't quite fit the image of the sort of man who would likely be best friends with someone like Brennon, who had been nothing but style so far. I wondered how long they'd known each other.

Once Steve had cleaned up most of his mess and returned to the couch and his earbuds, I set to work, digging in the pantry and fridge. I wanted something quick and easy but just complicated enough to get my mind off the girl in the photo and the strange friendship between Brennon and Steve. There wasn't much to work with—I remembered Brennon needed to go to the store—but I found some chicken thighs in the fridge and enough veggies to make a big enough salad for the both of us.

I tossed together a bunch of spices, coating the chicken and popping it into the oven to broil, and set about making a honey glaze for the chicken and chopping up the veggies. It would be simple, but at least it wasn't on the floor.

Just as I was pulling the now-glazed chicken from the oven, Steve suddenly appeared at my side and nearly scared me out of my wits. "Brennon didn't say you were a chef," he said.

I stared at him, my hand on my heart and incredibly grateful I managed to get the tray of chicken onto the stove before I dropped it all in fright. "What?" I gasped.

He nodded toward the chicken, a little wrinkle appearing between his eyebrows, as if he couldn't quite decide what to make of me. "It smells...impressive."

"I'm not a chef," I said, though a bit of heat spotted my cheeks at the idea.

Without a word, he reached into the drawer next to him, pulled out a knife and fork, and cut himself a bite, which he chewed slowly as if he were a judge on those cooking shows I probably spent too much time watching. My heart kept pounding, and I told myself it was because he had scared me. Not because I genuinely wanted to know what he thought about the chicken.

"This is delicious," he said finally, grabbing a couple of white plates from the cupboard above the counter and holding them out to me. "If you're not a chef, you should be. Where did you learn?"

Now he wanted to hold a conversation?

Dumping half the salad and a piece of chicken onto each plate, I followed him to the table and sat across from him, trying to figure out why his temperament was so different from how it had been earlier. He sat and picked up his fork, but he just watched me. Waiting.

Fine. "My mom," I said, rolling my eyes when he took a bite now that he was sure I would tell him. "She's a chef, and I spent a lot of years watching her work and learning from her."

"In Boston?"

I shook my head then realized he probably couldn't see me doing it. "No," I said, "in Vermont."

"You grew up there?" He paused eating when I didn't answer, his eyes searching for mine but coming up short. The wrinkle in his forehead deepened, joined by a downward tug of his lips beneath his thick beard. "What?"

"Why the inquisition?" I replied. It wasn't that I didn't want to tell him, and my childhood was a relatively happy one, especially since

Gordon Hastings hadn't been a part of it, but there was something about Steve that just wouldn't settle right. I couldn't figure out who he was, and men were generally pretty easy to read. Steve was not.

Shrugging, Steve pushed a carrot across his plate. "I don't need you to babysit me," he said.

"That wasn't an answer," I argued.

"I was getting to that."

"Get to it faster."

His frustration was almost tangible, and I couldn't help but smile. "I know Bren," he said. "If not you, he'll find someone else to stay with me. If I'm going to be stuck with you breathing down my neck, I might as well get to know you a little better."

The familiar phrase rankled, momentarily transporting me back to staff meetings I wasn't invited to, mainly so the men could complain about my management style. If I'd been a man, they would have done their jobs without encouragement, but because I was of the "lesser sex," I'd had to push them just to listen to simple requests. Yes, I was definitely glad to get out of that world, but I had fallen into something that was feeling eerily like the same thing on a smaller scale. At least Steve appreciated my cooking, though that thought alone seemed to shove feminism back a decade or two.

"Yes," I said finally, and his lips twitched upward. "I grew up in Vermont." And if he was going to ask questions, I had the right to ask my own. "Have you always been…" *Don't ask that, Lissa. Don't go there.* "Blind?"

His almost-smile immediately morphed back into a scowl. "What did Brennon tell you?"

I shrugged. "Not a lot."

With a sigh, he mirrored my movement without knowing it. "Not always," he said. "And I'm not blind. Technically. Cortical visual impairment. My eyes work fine. My brain does not."

Well that had to be a good sign, right? Eyes weren't exactly easy to repair, but brains could be manipulated. Right? Maybe I had that backwards. "Can they fix it?" I asked.

Steve just laughed once, shaking his head.

"I don't see why that's funny," I said.

"Well you wouldn't," he replied, rolling his eyes. "You're too busy seeing everything else."

Clever. "How did it happen?"

"I'm going to bed." Without another word, he stood and disappeared down the hallway, his door shutting behind him a second later.

I was deep in the middle of a horror movie I hadn't had time to watch before now when something touched my shoulder and made me shriek. I jumped up and was just about to launch into some strange ninja move when I realized it was Brennon standing behind me and trying his hardest not to laugh. He wasn't doing a very good job, but that was probably because I looked ridiculous with my hands in the air, ready to do some karate chopping.

"Brennon," I gasped as my heart kept racing.

He grinned. "You don't seem the type to scare so easily," he said and glanced at the TV to see what I was watching.

Normally I wasn't, which made my embarrassment that much worse. "Well, you know," I said, sinking back onto the couch before my legs gave out from under me. "First day in a strange place and all that." I hadn't realized how dark it had gotten in the room, and I was glad when Brennon flicked on the light overhead before he sat next to me.

He wasn't quite as close as I would have liked, especially because the movie kept playing, but he did take my hand, which made it easier to smile. "And how goes our invalid?" he asked.

I hadn't seen hide nor hair of Steve since lunch, though I had knocked on his door a couple of times to make sure he was still okay. He had responded each time with a growled, "Go away."

I sighed. "He's fine. I'm glad you're back, though." I had expected Brennon to be gone for only a couple of hours, but it was nearly eight o'clock. I wouldn't have thought looking after a grown man would be as exhausting as it had been today, and I badly needed the company of someone who actually wanted me around.

Though he still smiled, Brennon's brightness faded a bit. "I'm sorry I didn't make it back sooner," he said and scooted just a little nearer, which made my heart pick back up into its fast pace. "But at least I can honestly say I was thinking about you all day."

Well if that wasn't a way to make a girl blush, then I didn't know what was. Leaning closer, I tried not to look too eager as I said, "You were, huh?" I had done my very best *not* to think about Brennon, because if I thought too long on that kiss he'd given me before he rushed off to his office, it was particularly hard to concentrate on anything else. The man may have not had much game when it came to pick-up lines, but he sure knew how to kiss.

Lifting his hand to my neck, Brennon gave me the same smile that had drawn me into his apartment in the first place, and he moved in close enough to touch his nose to mine. "You, Lissa, make it extremely difficult for a man to concentrate on stock exchanges," he said. So maybe he *was* good at the lines too, but I was far more focused on the way he leaned in.

His kiss was even better than I expected, and it left me wondering how I could have gone my whole life without someone like Brennon Ashworth in my life. He made me feel like I was actually worth something. After so many exhausting years fighting my way through the male-dominated world of finance, being around a guy like Brennon was wildly refreshing. "You make it hard to concentrate on anything at all," I admitted.

Then, to my utter dismay, Brennon's phone started to ring. Sighing, he pulled it from his pocket and glanced at the screen for only a second before he answered the call. "What's wrong, Jake?" he said and was on his feet a moment later, moving to his bedroom and shutting the door behind him. The last words I caught were, "No, I told him to drop the shares as soon as possible," which meant apparently he wasn't done with work just yet.

Disappointed, I settled back onto the couch to watch the rest of the movie, though I wasn't sure I understood anything of what was going on. Both in the movie and in my life. Today had been chaotic enough, and tomorrow I would have to start thinking about where the rest of my life was headed now that I was jobless and directionless. The future, as much as I hated to think about it, was looking rather bleak.

CHAPTER SEVEN

A girl could only do nothing for so long before she cracked. True, reading wasn't nothing, but for some reason I couldn't seem to focus on any of the books I pulled from Brennon's shelf. Brennon was probably partially to blame, giving me a knee-weakening kiss before heading to the office early that morning. In a surprising act of chivalry, he'd offered up his bed to me and slept on the couch, coming into the bedroom only to grab a shirt and slacks to change into. I had tried to argue that I had a whole apartment just across the hall I could use, but he told me he wanted to spend every moment he could with me and begged me to stay at his place. How could I argue with that?

While I was a little disappointed that he'd been so exhausted after his ridiculously long phone call with whoever Jake was and had gone to bed soon after, I was optimistic that tonight we could spend some real time together.

Until then, I had to find some way to entertain myself.

Steve was no help. He spent the morning on the couch with his earbuds in, whatever music he had on drowning out the rest of the world. Including me. I almost envied his ability to do absolutely nothing for so long, but seeing him on that couch all day made me feel sorry for Brennon, who clearly did all the work around the apartment. How was it they were such good friends when they were two completely different people?

When my stomach started demanding lunch, I rummaged through the many cupboards again only to discover I'd used most of the food for last night's dinner.

"Could you stop?" Steve said suddenly.

I turned to face him, letting another cupboard door fall closed. "Stop what?"

He winced when it shut. "I'm blind," he said. "I'm not deaf. You're being ridiculously loud."

Well I'm sorry for trying to keep you from starving, I kept myself from saying. Going full bitter wasn't going to help either of us. "What is it you do all day, anyway?" I asked, wishing he could see my raised eyebrow.

His expression was completely blank as he said, "I'm doing it."

"You've got to be kidding," I mumbled, pulling my hair back with the fingers of one hand. God give me the patience. "We need food," I announced, watching his expression shift to confusion. "Which means I have to go to the store." He immediately started frowning. "Which means you, my friend, have to come with me."

"Nah." He pulled his phone right up in front of his face and squinted at the screen. As soon as he found what he was looking for, he settled back against the pillows on the couch.

"Yeah," I replied and grabbed his arm to pull him to his feet. If he'd been any bigger, I wouldn't have been able to move him, since he was several inches taller than me, but he was a lot lighter than his clothes implied and practically flew upwards with my tug. He grabbed my shoulder as his swollen knee gave out, but even that barely pushed me. How thin was this guy?

"I'll be fine on my own," he said, trying to free himself.

I linked our arms and pulled him toward the door. "I'm sure you would be," I replied. "Now, where are your shoes?"

He mumbled something about them being by the front door. He mumbled all the way down the elevator ride. He mumbled when I shoved him into the passenger seat of Brennon's car, and I half expected him to make a run for it. I *was* curious how far he'd get without being able to see, but I wasn't about to test it. My goal was to keep the guy safe, not get him hit by another car.

I quickly searched for the nearest grocery store and plugged it into the GPS, and then I took a deep breath to calm my nerves as I pulled onto the street. I was grateful Brennon had trusted me with the keys when he said he was taking the bus this morning, but I never drove in Boston. It had been almost a year since I'd even sat behind the wheel, so it was probably a good thing Steve wouldn't be able to see my nerves or comment on how slow I was going. As long as no one ran straight into us, we'd be fine.

The silence, however, was not going to make anything easier. "My cousin was hit by a car once," I said to make conversation. *Why in the world would I say something like* that?

Steve gave me a deadpan look that clearly said, *Really?* Of all the topics I could have chosen, I had to pick that one.

Oh well. "Yeah," I said. "He was fifteen. Knocked him right into a hedge. And it took him four years before he was brave enough to take Driver's Ed. True story."

Muttering something that sounded like, "You're an idiot," Steve turned his head to look out the window.

So maybe my conversation skills could use some work. "Sorry," I admitted, though I smiled to myself. "It's been a while since I talked to anyone about something that wasn't money-related."

"I can tell."

"Then why don't you pick the topic?"

"Why don't we sit in silence?"

I huffed, gripping the steering wheel a little tighter than was probably necessary. We were only halfway to the store, and it was only the first full day of my week-long vigil. How long could I keep this up, really? Maybe I could convince Brennon to take a day off so we could tackle this whole Steve thing together.

"Stop the car," Steve said suddenly, and I nearly slammed on the brakes before realizing it would probably be safer to pull over instead.

"What's wrong?" I asked as soon as we were stationary, turning to him in a panic. Was he dying? I didn't have any medical experience, and I could barely get a Band-aid to stay in place longer than an hour. Should I call 911?

"Coffee," Steve said.

Halfway through searching for the nearest hospital on my phone, I looked up at him in absolute confusion. *His head injury.* It was addling his brain, and he was completely losing it. Was that still something 911 worthy? I had no idea. "What?" I gasped.

He very nearly smiled, probably hearing the panic in my voice. "Coffee," he said again, tapping his knuckle against the glass next to him.

I glanced out his window, and to my surprise we were parked right outside a bustling coffee shop called *Indiana Brews*. I had so many questions, but the first was, "You saw that?"

"I smelled that," he corrected. "Brennon has the worst taste in coffee, and he thinks I don't know the difference just because I can't see the label. Come on." And with that, he opened his door and stepped onto the curb.

The man *did not* just send me into a panic because he wanted some coffee. "Hey!" I said, still strapped into the car. He was nearly to the door as someone held it open for him, so I fought to free myself of the seatbelt and stumbled inside after him, barely registering the bittersweet scent of coffee lingering in the air around me.

I only got two steps into the cute little shop when I heard a surprised, "Lissa?"

My eyes wide, I turned and found Catherine's cousin, Matthew, staring at me from where he sat reading at one of the little wooden tables that littered the shop's cozy lobby. Never mind he recognized me at all, but recognizing me when I was supposed to be back in Boston left me a little stunned as I stood there. Sure, we had talked during the drive from the airport, but he'd been watching the road the whole time, and with all the attention he gave Indie, I doubted he had ever gotten a good look at my face.

"Lissa!" another voice chimed in, and suddenly his girlfriend had her arms around me in a strangling hold. "What are you doing here?"

I was about to ask the same thing when it clicked. *Indiana Brews.* "You own a coffee shop?" I asked Indie, both surprised and amazed. It was an adorable little shop, with lots of wood and Edison bulbs and a very hipster feel to it. Exactly the sort of place I would have expected to see in San Francisco. And by the looks of the shop's many customers milling around the place, even though it was early afternoon, it was the place to be.

Her eyes bright and her smile wide, Indie shook her head. "He owns it," she corrected, nodding toward Matthew.

Matthew just rolled his eyes and took a sip of what I was pretty sure was hot chocolate, not coffee. It even had mini marshmallows bobbing at the top. "What's it going to take to stop you from saying that?" he asked, and then he subconsciously rubbed his empty ring finger with his thumb, unknowingly telling me he knew exactly what would convince Indie to consider the shop hers. I wondered how long it would be before he popped the question.

"What are you doing here?" Indie asked without giving Matthew a response. "I thought you were heading back to Boston yesterday."

"I was," I said, "but then I..." My stomach flipped. Oh crap, where was Steve? Spinning a full 180 degrees, I breathed a sigh of relief when I found him staring at the menu on the wall with his scowl growing deeper by the second. Even if he could see a little bit, there was no way he could possibly read that. "Hey," I said, turning back to Indie, "do you have a handheld menu by chance?"

Indie procured one from the pocket of her apron, and I quickly brought it over to Steve, stuffing it into his hands without preamble. He stared at it, and then at me, and then he looked back at the menu as the little wrinkle between his eyebrows grew deeper than I'd seen it yet. "Thanks," he muttered, sounding more surprised than anything.

"Um." Indie suddenly grabbed my hand, pulling me back toward Matthew's table with way too excited a look on her face. "Who's that?"

I knew she eagerly awaited my answer—even Matthew looked up from his book with interest—but I glanced back at Steve and couldn't help but grin. He held the menu only an inch from his face and looked somewhat cross-eyed. But he also almost smiled, which was a much better look for him than his usual scowl.

"Friend of a friend," I said, turning back to the couple a second too late to catch the bulk of the look they shared. "What?"

Matthew pretended to be immersed in his book again, but Indie smiled. "He's cute," she said. And if she kept talking at this volume, I would have to end this conversation real quick.

"He's annoying," I replied quietly. "He just got out of the hospital and needs someone with him at all times, and I had some vacation days to spend, so I volunteered."

"That's not a vacation," Matthew said with a pitying grimace.

Indie slapped her hand against his shoulder. "What would you know?" she asked him. "You haven't had a vacation since you were seventeen."

"Anything is a vacation when you work where I work," I replied before Matthew offered up whatever witty response he came up with. "It's just nice to get away." I could see the concern building in their eyes, which meant I hadn't hidden the bitterness that crept up whenever I thought about my old job, so I glanced back to see Steve being handed his coffee and gave the pair of them a wave. "Gotta run," I said, "but it was good to see you."

"Don't be a stranger!" Indie called after me. "Stop by any time."

I linked my arm with Steve's and pulled him a little faster than necessary toward the door, just in case Indie decided to offer some sort of assistance I didn't need. After the way she'd talked to me at Seth's wedding, I had a feeling she was the sort of person who offered up help at the slightest provocation, and Matthew was probably the same way. I didn't need them halting their lives just because I'd impulsively made some questionable decisions.

We got all the way to the sidewalk before Steve slipped from my grip and glanced back at the shop. "Who was that?" he asked. Why was he so interested?

"No one," I replied and opened his door for him.

He didn't move. "She sounded nice. He did too. Why run?"

"Because they're going to try to help me," I said. "Just get in the car."

He did as instructed, but the second I sat in my own seat, he turned to me and raised one eyebrow. "Help you in the same way you're trying to help me?" he said. What was that supposed to mean?

"I don't…" I stopped myself from fighting back. Steve seemed like the sort of person who would keep pushing an issue unless it concerned him, and it was a little unnerving how much of myself I saw in him. "They're Catherine's family," I explained quietly and pulled out into the street, back en route to the grocery store. "Which means they're Seth's family. Which means they're my family."

"Curse those pesky families trying to make sure you're looked after and cared for," he muttered into his coffee cup.

If only he could see my glare. "They're just a little overbearing," I argued.

"Because someone worrying about you is just the worst."

That wasn't what I meant, and he knew it. "I don't appreciate the sarcasm," I grumbled.

"Then don't ask for it." There it was again, a complete change of mood for no apparent reason. Steve was exhausting, and I had no idea how Brennon had put up with him for so long.

Steve was silent the whole time at the grocery store, simply following behind me with his hands in his pockets as I pushed the cart and occasionally grunting when I asked him if he would eat certain things. He didn't say a word on the drive home either, and I had a feeling the trend would continue once we got back to the apartment, since he didn't give any indications otherwise.

I deserved his annoyance. At least a little. I shouldn't have complained that people cared about me, especially people who barely knew me, but that was half the problem. They didn't know me. They didn't know what I was capable of or what I'd been through, and they assumed I couldn't take care of myself even though I'd been doing that for a long time. Even after Indie said it had taken her a while to get used to the Davenports, she obviously fit right in with them because she had Matthew. Catherine had Seth. Lanna had Adam.

And I had a feeling they would likely keep pestering me until I had my own outrageously perfect man on my arm. Indie hadn't exactly been subtle when she said Steve was cute.

Brennon brought home takeout for dinner, which was great since I wasn't in the mood to cook and I honestly couldn't tell if Steve was in the mood to eat, seeing as he went straight into his room after we got back from the store and hadn't emerged from his headphone haze since. I was flipping through TV channels, certifiably bored, and a wave of warmth passed over me the moment Brennon stepped through the door.

"You're back," I breathed, letting that knowledge lift some of the gloominess that had settled over me.

Brennon glanced toward the bedrooms as he set the food on the table then settled next to me on the couch. "How's Steve?" he asked, slipping his hand into mine.

"Steve's fine," Steve himself answered from his room, his frustration clear in his voice.

"Steve's in a mood," I added in a whisper and ran my fingers along Brennon's jaw. He hadn't taken the time to shave that morning, and I was liking the scruff.

Smiling, he scooted a little closer, turning his head so my fingers brushed his lips. "Steve's always in a mood lately."

I had a lot I wanted to say, but Brennon seriously made it hard to focus with the way his kisses trailed down my hand to my wrist. I settled with the most important. "I don't think he likes me very much," I said. "Maybe someone else would…"

Sighing—apparently I killed *our* mood—Brennon shook his head. "If he's in a mood now, he'd been even worse with a stranger."

Based on what I knew about the guy, I didn't doubt it, but that didn't help my problem. "But *I'm* a stranger."

Leaning in, Brennon just barely touched his lips to mine, teasing me with a kiss meant to disarm my argument. It was working. I pulled in closer, deepening the embrace until my head spun. "I'd be okay if we changed that," he whispered against my lips, and then I was lost to his touch.

"Food," Steve said suddenly and loudly as he passed the couch on his way to the table.

I almost laughed, my face burning as Brennon's grin nearly pulled me back in. "Food," I whispered back, and Brennon did laugh, helping me to my feet so we could join Steve. Though how I was supposed to focus on Kung Pao Chicken, I had no idea. Not after a kiss like that. Maybe Brennon wasn't "the one" my new family probably hoped I would find, and maybe this thing between us wouldn't last. Particularly because the man apparently didn't believe in love. I was starting to wonder how true that really was, based on how easily he fell into rhythm with me. But I liked him—a lot—and I wasn't about to douse the flame just because there was a chance it might rain.

In a few days, Steve would be fine to spend his days alone like he wanted, and Brennon and I could figure out whatever this was. For now, I would just have to enjoy his surreptitious smiles across the table and hope they lasted.

CHAPTER EIGHT

Morning brought with it the smell of bacon. I loved bacon. "But why so early?" I moaned as my stomach rumbled, effectively ruining any chance I had of falling back asleep for an hour or two. I had no idea how Brennon managed to stay up late watching a movie with me and then get up early enough to cook bacon before work, but I envied him the ability. I had never been a morning person, something all the tabloid magazines had been sure to exploit back when the world had thought Seth and I were dating.

"Oh, come on," I mumbled and pressed a pillow over my face. I had nearly forgotten about those terrifying months of paparazzi hoping to figure out who the elusive Lissa Montgomery was who had stolen the heart of America's favorite bachelor. They all thought I was some glamorous millionaire who would help raise Seth's already ridiculously high status until we were the ultimate power couple and out running the world one smile at a time. *I'm his sister, you idiots*, I finally told them, and the tabloid tales thankfully stopped there.

Did Brennon know about that brief part of my life? He certainly seemed like the type to pay attention to the latest gossip. Maybe I'd subtly ask him about it over breakfast, just to see if he, like the rest of the world, had fallen into a temporary lapse of judgment. Like when one magazine decided I was beauty and grace and marrying Mr. United States, all the common folk apparently in agreement and cheering me on for a very short period of time.

"Wake up, Lissa!" I scolded myself, too lost in my thoughts to remember there was bacon out in the main room. Bacon and Brennon.

Yawning, I trudged down the hallway and tried to somewhat straighten my hair with my fingers so I wasn't an absolute mess. Sure, the man had seen me drunk and nearly had to endure me vomiting on his shoes, but that didn't mean I wouldn't put in a little effort. I wanted to keep him around, not scare him off, and I could only get so lucky.

"How is it stock brokers have unlimited energy?" I asked as I approached the kitchen counter.

Steve looked up from the two boxes he held, and my heart skipped a beat in embarrassment. Steve. Not Brennon. Steve was making bacon? "I have no idea," he muttered, "and it's a little terrifying when you get the bigshot going. Which one of these is pancake mix?"

I glanced at the two identical boxes. "Uh, both," I said.

His eyes very nearly focused on me as he stared in my direction, his brow pulling together in that single wrinkle. "Both," he repeated. "Are you telling me you bought two boxes of pancake mix?"

"I happen to like pancakes," I replied and reached for the plate of bacon, taking a bite of the expertly crispy meat. The man knew what he was doing. "You're making breakfast," I pointed out, my statement almost a question. So far, I'd only seen him eat cereal, and that included both breakfast and lunch. The guy wasn't exactly Gordon Ramsay.

"And they say *I'm* blind," he muttered to himself as he carefully measured the mix into a measuring cup. "You know, I did manage to feed myself before you appeared." With the way his clothes hung loose on his thin frame, I wasn't sure how true that was.

I watched him mix the pancake batter, sloshing a bunch out the side of the bowl, and though my instinct was to hurry forward and help him, I just sat at the kitchen table and watched him knock over the box of mix with his elbow.

"Oops," he said as the mix spilled across the counter. *Oops?* That was not the word I expected him to say, not after some of the things I'd heard come out of his mouth. Something was different about today, and I was starting to get seriously concerned about this man's mood swings. He was almost happy as he successfully managed to flip a pancake without tossing it out of the pan. I wondered...

"How did you lose your sight?" I asked softly, and his movement slowed. Would he answer?

"An accident," he said after a moment.

I didn't ask any follow up questions because I didn't want to push him too far, but it was something. An accident. One that likely caused a head injury, if my little bit of research into cortical visual impairment was correct. That, and what the doctor had been saying at the hospital.

"How much can you see?" I continued. That, I figured, wasn't too prying of a question, and it would help me know how much he actually needed my help.

He took a slow breath, subconsciously working his spoon through the pancake batter as he thought about my question. "Close things," he said quietly. "Bright colors. Some shapes. It changes from day to day, but..."

"I was reading about it," I told him. "Sometimes your sight can come back."

He almost smiled, but it was more of an ironic upturn of his lips. "It's been two years," he replied. "I don't think it's ever coming back."

Well not with that attitude. Maybe I shouldn't have pushed it, but I moved into my next question in my quest to figure out who this blind man was. "So why the pancakes?" I asked.

"You happen to like pancakes," he replied without missing a beat, and that almost-smile of his grew.

I grinned, definitely preferring this happy version of Steve to the grumpy pessimist. Maybe this week wouldn't be so bad after all. "Come on."

"Consider it a thank you," he said and placed a plate of food in front of me. It all looked delicious, and I had a hard time keeping my focus on the man and not the food. I had to capitalize on his chattiness before it disappeared.

"Thank me for what?" I asked.

"Yesterday." He sat opposite me with his own plate, the confused wrinkle deep between his eyebrows as he gazed at his food. "Bren would have read the menu to me."

He was thanking me for giving him the handheld menu? "I just figured that was the easiest," I said. I hadn't even thought about how annoying it must have been to have people do everything for him. Maybe that was why he was so grumpy, and he needed those little victories to keep his spirits up. Losing his sight had to have been a hard blow, and I was amazed he had gotten this far more or less intact.

"Are you actually going to eat this time?" I asked, frowning a little as I looked more closely at how poorly most of his clothes fit. Either Brennon was really bad at remembering to go grocery shopping, or there was something more at play here. I worried it was the latter.

Steve stopped pushing eggs around his plate and looked up at me in confusion. "What?"

If I was going to look after this guy for the next week, I might as well do a good job. "Last night," I said. "You barely ate anything."

"I ate," he argued.

"Three bites of chicken doesn't count."

"I ate *your* chicken."

"That was the day before and also doesn't count. And before you say you eat cereal, I'm not sure Cocoa Puffs actually counts as a valid food option."

I was pretty sure he didn't know what to do with that comment, and he just sat there with his mouth slightly open, extremely focused in my direction. Brennon probably never noticed how much he pretended to eat by moving things around and taking small bites, so Steve had probably gotten used to doing it. Why he would avoid eating, I wasn't sure, but I guessed it had something to do with the accident that made him blind. I would have to see if Brennon had any pictures of Steve before the accident to be positive. But for now, I had to make sure the guy ate some actual breakfast.

Still in his stare-down, Steve slowly speared a clump of egg with his fork and stuck it in his mouth, making a show of chewing and swallowing. If I wasn't afraid he would stop, I'd probably start laughing at the ridiculousness of it all. Instead, I just grinned and hoped he really couldn't see me all that well.

He didn't quite have the energy he'd had before, but I hoped he would still be up for talking if I asked any of the million questions that had piled up in my head since meeting the guy. I waited until he'd had a couple of bites of pancake, and then I said, "Why are you so against getting a dog, anyway? I'm pretty sure Brennon wouldn't mind having one around."

He shrugged as he chewed some bacon. "It seems like overkill, if you ask me."

Interesting. "Why?" I asked. "A dog could help you cross the street, at the very least, and they're trained to—"

"Do you know how much one of those things costs?" Steve asked, dropping his fork as he stared toward me. "Not to mention the waiting list, and the training, and the city ordinances, and the fact that I don't actually need one."

I highly doubted that last one, but I had a feeling this was an argument I wouldn't win. He had clearly looked into it and decided it wasn't an option, even if he thought he could use the help. Why couldn't he just say he had tried instead of getting so uppity? Steve was an enigma for sure, and a large part of me really wanted to try to figure him out. After all, what else was I going to do all week?

I had to focus back on priorities, though, and make sure he ate.

"These pancakes are delicious," I said and made a show of taking a bite.

He got the hint, though he rolled his eyes as he followed suit. He grumbled something in between bites that sounded like, "You're worse than Brennon," and I took that as a compliment.

"So why did you get up so early?" I asked him. I was still tempted to go back to sleep, but since Steve was up and about, that probably wasn't an option.

"You're just full of questions this morning," he grumbled back, pushing a bit of pancake around the syrup on his plate.

"Questions that need answers," I replied.

"I couldn't sleep."

"Was it my snoring?" I asked. Steve raised an eyebrow, and I grinned. "Brennon can't stand it apparently, so he sleeps on the couch."

"Brennon is too much of a gentleman for his own good," Steve mumbled.

Yeah, and I loved that about him. "Why are you so determined to corrupt him?" I asked. One of the first things Steve had said to me was about how disappointed he was that Brennon wasn't a pig, and that didn't exactly do any favors for Steve's character.

Rolling his eyes again, he took another bite of eggs. "You can't honestly think I actually want Bren to be a tool, can you? He's so good that he makes the rest of us look bad. He's been that way since the day I met him freshman year, and if I didn't love the guy, I would seriously hate him."

"So you're trying to take down the competition a peg," I surmised. Not that Steve could really compete at this point with his perpetual grumpiness, so I couldn't see why he would even bother. Besides, Brennon Ashworth was in a league of his own. "Not gonna lie, I'm having a hard time convincing myself Brennon is even real."

Snorting a laugh, Steve shook his head. "You and me both," he muttered. "I've known the man for thirteen years, and I still haven't figured him out."

This was probably a terrible idea, but I couldn't help myself. "You wouldn't happen to know who the girl is in the picture on his nightstand, would you?" I said then winced, waiting for Steve to tell me it was his girlfriend, even though I would be stupid to think Brennon could be the sort of guy who cheated on someone. The picture was too old for that, anyway.

But Steve frowned. "Picture on his nightstand? No idea. I don't think I've ever seen him put a picture anywhere aside from one of his parents. What does she look like?"

Honestly, I'd been avoiding the picture ever since that first time I saw it, but that didn't mean the girl wasn't fully ingrained in my memory. Clearly she was important to Brennon, but I had no idea what that meant. "She looks a lot like me," I said with a shrug.

"Because that helps me out so much," he replied roughly, and then he set his fork on his plate and stood. Apparently the conversation was over. Maybe one of these days I would teach him how to actually end a conversation instead of just walking away. But at least he had stayed long enough to eat all his food, so I was making progress, if only a little.

"Thanks for breakfast," I told him. "I can clean up, if you'd like."

He paused near the couch, turning his head so one ear was pointing back at me. "That would be nice," he admitted quietly. "I have a bit of a headache, so I should probably lie down for a bit."

"A headache?" I couldn't fully disguise my worry, and Steve definitely heard it.

"I'm fine," he said, obviously annoyed as he made his way to his bedroom and shut the door.

Hopefully that didn't mean extra grumpy Steve was back, but it *did* mean I had another morning all to myself, and I had no idea how I was going to stave off the boredom this time. At least I finally had a mess to clean up in the kitchen. And maybe I could make up a menu for the rest of the week too. While I didn't know for sure if Steve really did have a problem with eating, he was right about eating the other night when I made the chicken. If I could keep making him more dishes like that, things that surprised and excited him, maybe I could get some meat on his bones.

And maybe I could get some life back into his life. I may not have had my own life put together anymore, but maybe I could help him out with his. Between the two of us, at least one of us deserved something good.

I didn't realize I'd fallen asleep until my phone woke me up, Brennon's name on the screen and my heart skipping a little faster in excitement. Setting aside the book I had tried—and apparently failed—reading, I sat up on Brennon's bed and lifted the phone to my ear.

"Hey," I said, smiling to myself.

"Hey," he replied, and I could almost hear his own smile. "I was sitting here eating lunch all by myself like usual, and I decided I didn't want to wait until tonight to talk to you."

I felt very proud for managing to keep my squeal an internal one. He was seriously good at this sweet talk thing. "Is that so?" I asked. "Am I really so fun to talk to?"

"So much better than these bozos here at the office. All they can talk about is baseball and money."

"You realize you're saying that to a financial analyst, right? And a Red Sox fan."

He laughed, making me so glad I didn't have to wait until tonight either. I didn't know much about Brennon Ashworth, but I did know I liked him. Probably a little too much, even with that photo of him and the girl sitting on the nightstand next to me. Whoever she was, she probably didn't get lunchtime phone calls. That was good enough for me.

"Former financial analyst," he corrected. "I can't do anything about your taste in sports, but the offer still stands to come work with me, you know."

That idea was a lot more tempting than it had been on Sunday, but I really didn't have a strong background in stocks. I doubted I was truly qualified, even if he had some sort of influence in his office. Besides, I wanted something more fulfilling. That was the point. "Thanks," I told him, "but I'll leave that to you. I have to find my new dream before I can make any decisions like that."

"You are an inspiration, Lissa. I wish I had that kind of courage. You know, to wait for the right thing instead of going for the first choice I come across."

My heart sank a little, though I wasn't sure why, and I glanced at the photograph again. At some point I would have to ask Brennon about her, though I didn't know how long it would take me to work up the courage. For all I knew, she was the love of his life and had disappeared.

Just as I was about to shift the conversation to an easier topic, a shadow crossed the doorway—Steve heading out into the main room. "Hey," I said into the phone, quickly scooting off the bed so I could follow, "I'm so glad you called me, and tonight feels like a really long time away, but I should make some lunch before Steve makes another mess out in the kitchen."

"Another mess?" Brennon sounded worried. "What did he do this morning?"

Something I never would have expected, but I had a feeling Brennon wouldn't consider pancakes an accomplishment. "Nothing," I replied quickly. "I'll see you later."

Hurrying down the hall, I slid a bit on the hardwood and to Steve's side just as he pulled open a cupboard in search of food. He cursed in alarm and stepped back, knocking his shoulder into some hanging wine glasses beneath the cupboard and sending one of them crashing down to the edge of the counter, where it immediately shattered. His next step back to steady himself brought his socked foot down onto a piece of glass, so he lifted it back up but managed to lose his footing, slipping and landing on his rear end with a grunt as his phone went flying, bringing his earbuds with it.

"What is wrong with you, woman!" he shouted as soon as the proverbial dust settled.

I clapped my hand over my mouth, partly in horror for causing all of that but mostly to stop myself from laughing. "I'm so sorry," I whispered down to him. "I thought for sure you heard me."

"Headphones," he grunted, still sitting where he'd landed as his whole face burned red.

Poor guy. He probably still wasn't used to anyone being at the apartment with him, and I'd gone and scared the bejeebers out of him. "How did even you know I was here?" I asked, still on the verge of laughing. Could he have been any more over-the-top with his reaction? Probably not.

Grabbing the counter above him, he pulled himself to his feet and quickly distanced himself from the broken glass and more importantly me. "Movement," he said roughly, wrapping an arm around his ribs.

"Seriously, what is wrong with you?"

I just shook my head. "So many things," I said. "What were you listening to that was so enthralling?"

He glanced around him, likely searching for his lost phone, and I quickly moved around the counter and scooped it up for him, though he jumped again when I appeared on his other side. "Stop *doing* that," he begged, though he relaxed a bit when I set the phone in his hands and managed a mumbled, "Thanks."

"I'm going to clean this up," I told him, "and you're going to sit down while I make some lunch. It's probably safer that way."

Apparently he agreed, because he headed straight for the couch. His limp was worse, I noticed, his injured knee probably damaged more by his sudden fall in the kitchen, and every breath seemed to cause him pain as his bruised ribs protested his hard landing. He'd been so good at hiding his pain before that I'd almost forgotten he'd been hit by a car just a couple of days ago.

"Sorry," I said again, this time more sincere. "I didn't scare you on purpose."

"I know," he grunted.

Finding a hand broom beneath the kitchen sink, I quickly swept up all the offending glass and dumped it in the garbage. Then I swept again, just in case. Brennon and I might have caught a piece or two before we stepped on it, but there was no way Steve would have been able to avoid it. Hopefully he hadn't cut himself when stepping on it before and his reaction was just reflex, not because of actual pain. I'd done enough damage already.

"Books," Steve said when I straightened back up once I was convinced the floor was glass-free.

I pulled my eyebrows together. "What?"

He held up his phone and the earbuds dangling from it, though he hadn't put them back in his ears. "I listen to books. As many as I can."

Oh. "Because you can't read them," I realized out loud. So it wasn't music he wasted time with, but books, which weren't a waste of time at all.

Nodding, he wrapped the earbuds around his phone then set it on the couch next to him. "I miss reading," he admitted, and I felt a surge of pity for him. "Audiobooks are great, but they take too much time. Speed listening makes me dizzy."

I knew very little about Steve Evans, but suddenly I wanted to know everything about pre-accident Steve and the life he lost when he lost his sight. "What are you listening to today?"

Hesitating, he massaged his knee for a moment then muttered, "Machiavelli again."

Did he just say *again*? "Naturally," I replied, glad he couldn't see my awe. "I suppose you've listened to all the greats and classics, then?"

"Most of them," he said without a pause.

Of course he had. "What's your favorite?" Forget about lunch; I wanted to know what sort of book a man like him valued above all others. But because I'd already added enough trauma to the man's life, I quickly started grabbing things to make sandwiches as I waited for his response.

"I'm not sure I have a favorite," he said after giving it a moment's thought. "Everything is worth learning, and after a year of listening to anything I can get my hands on..." He stopped himself, bowing his head. What was he hiding? Better yet, what had he been doing during the first year after his accident? He said it happened two years ago, and I was pretty sure he knew I caught the inconsistency.

I couldn't help but wonder how much Brennon knew about what his friend had gone through over the last two years. With all the time he spent at his office, I wasn't sure he knew much at all.

"I noticed you were reading," Steve said after a moment of silence, the lightness in his voice forced and strained. But I would let him change the subject, because at least he was talking. I would take any improvement in his mood over the silent treatment. "Though it didn't exactly sound like a page turner," he added.

"*The 7 Habits of Highly Effective People*," I replied, "though I keep falling asleep."

He brightened just a bit, sitting up a little straighter in interest. "It's a good one," he said. "Maybe it's easier to listen to. I have it, if you..."

Putting his sandwich on a plate, I crossed over to the couch and announced, "I'm sitting down," before dropping onto the cushions and setting the plate in his hands.

"Ha," he said but immediately took to examining the sandwich, lifting it close enough to his face to both see and smell it. I practically held my breath while I waited for him to either say something or start eating it. "What is this?" he finally asked, his wrinkled brow mixed with interest. "Salmon?"

"And dill," I said. "It's better with a different bread like pumpernickel, but I didn't think to buy some when we were at the store yesterday, so you'll have to endure some good old-fashioned whole wheat."

He took a bite—a rather large one, I noticed with a smile—and chewed for a moment, even closing his eyes, probably so he could completely focus on the taste. "Is that lemon?" he asked in surprise. "On a sandwich?"

I couldn't help but grin as he took another large bite. Maybe fattening him up wouldn't be as hard as I thought. "It gives it a little flair, don't you think?"

"Flair," he repeated, shaking his head. "Here," he added and handed me his phone. "If you want to listen to it. After you get your own lunch, of course."

Huh. Steve Evans was certainly full of surprises, and I honestly couldn't have said what it was exactly that brought my next sentence out of my mouth: "How about we listen to it together?"

It caught him so off guard that he smeared a bit of cream cheese in his beard when he turned to me. "Together?" he repeated, and I couldn't decide if he was annoyed or pleased. Hopefully the second.

Returning to the kitchen, I fought to keep my smile out of my voice. "Sure," I said. "Then you can explain anything I don't understand, and I don't have to feel bad for completely taking your books away from you for the afternoon."

"Worse things have happened," he muttered. When I glanced back at him, he sat on the couch with the smallest of smiles, the first real one I'd seen since that morning I met him.

As soon as I had a sandwich to munch on and Steve had a napkin, we settled side by side on the couch, each with an earbud, and started the book.

CHAPTER NINE

I didn't notice Brennon until he was practically right in front of us. Though my heart skittered with alarm—suddenly I wondered when I had started getting spooked so easily—it quickly pattered into an easy rhythm of familiar excitement at the sight of Brennon's steely blue eyes and altogether handsomeness. "Brennon!" I greeted and pulled myself free from the earbud telling me to work to understand an individual's interests and needs.

Brennon accepted my hug but only with one arm, and I found myself sinking into disappointment until I realized what he held in his left hand.

"Flowers?" I asked eagerly. I couldn't even remember the last time someone had given me flowers at all, let alone a dozen roses. For a man who didn't believe in love, he certainly understood the art of romance.

Smiling warmly, Brennon held the bouquet out to me then leaned forward to place a lingering kiss on my cheek. "You had me distracted all day," he said softly, and his eyes twinkled enough that I wished I could say the same. Steve was right about the book, and I was so eager to keep listening and learning more that I had barely registered how dark it had gotten. The day had slipped away without me even noticing.

"Thank you for the flowers," I replied, knowing it didn't at all compare to his comment. *I should add something more.* "I'm glad you're home."

"So am I." Slipping his hands around my waist, Brennon pulled me close.

I breathed in his scent, eager for his touch and his kiss, but then my eyes caught a large plastic bag on the counter. "What's that?" I asked, wincing when I realized how quickly I broke his intense gaze.

With a sigh, Brennon smiled a little and stepped back. "I brought dinner," he said.

"Oh."

His face immediately fell, disappointment darkening his eyes as he said, "Sorry, I should have asked. You were so happy when I brought food last night, so I thought maybe... Do you even like Thai?"

It wasn't that. Thai food was delicious. But Steve had barely eaten our Chinese the night before, and I worried he would have the same reaction to more takeout and simply pretend to eat. He needed something more homemade, something surprising enough to help him forget his hunger strike whether or not he was even aware he had one.

"It's great," I said finally, trying to sound excited. "Really."

"What I really wanted," Brennon continued, taking my hand, "was to take you to my favorite restaurant across town, but..."

But someone had to stay with Steve. I turned to ask Steve how he felt about Thai—I would make him something else if I had to—but I only caught sight of his elbow as he limped into the hallway and disappeared. So Grumpy Steve was back, was he?

"I'll be right back," I said and grabbed one of the food containers, not even caring what it was. With a fork in hand, I hurried over to Steve's room and knocked on the door, waiting only half a second before pushing my way inside.

"Let yourself in," he mumbled from where he stood in the middle of the floor.

I glanced around only long enough to take in the mounds of clothes and garbage littered around the room, and then I stepped over a pair of jeans and placed the food in his hands. "Eat this," I ordered.

"Excuse me?"

"Eat it," I repeated clearly. "Your friend and roommate was kind enough to bring it home, and you're going to eat the whole thing."

He'd pretty much lost his grumpiness and simply looked confused as he stood there, the paper box in one hand and a fork in the other like some king with his orb and scepter. "Or?" he wondered.

"Or I'll come in here and force feed it to you," I replied. "And don't think I won't."

He looked down at the box then gently pried it open, staring at its contents from a few different angles before returning his unfocused gaze to me. "This is just a box of rice," he said, and the corner of his mouth twitched.

Oops. "Fine," I replied. "I'm going to go back and get you some actual food, and you're going to eat *that.*"

By the time I got back with some curry—and felt the heat of embarrassment under Brennon's inquiring gaze—Steve still hadn't moved, though his mood seemed to have only improved in the few seconds I was gone. "Here," I told him. "Now promise me I won't have to come back in here to make sure you didn't hide it under the bed instead of eating it."

He grinned. And for a second, I completely forgot what I'd even said. The man had a *smile.* "Do you really think I would do that?" he asked quietly.

"Or throw it out the window," I replied, stumbling over the words a bit. He didn't even *have* a window in his room. "I assume you can get creative when you put your mind to it. Are we going to have a problem?"

In answer, Steve stabbed his fork into the box, pulled out an enormous piece of chicken, and stuffed the whole thing into his mouth.

"Good," I said, closing the door behind me and taking a second to recover from that smile. Maybe all wasn't lost for Steve Evans.

Brennon was on the couch now, his tie undone and his suit jacket draped over the arm. Though he leaned on his knees, he straightened up when I sat next to him, and he slid his arm around me, pulling me close. "I thought he'd gotten over that," he said.

It took me a second to figure out what that meant. "You knew about the eating problem?" I asked in alarm. Then why hadn't he done anything about it?

Shrugging, Brennon suddenly looked exhausted. "That first year after the accident, I was really worried about him. It's why I asked him to move in here and sell his house. So I could keep an eye on him."

I couldn't help but turn to the hallway, trying to imagine what Steve was doing right then. Was he eating, like he agreed to do? Or was he figuring out a way to make it look like he had? "What happened to him?" I asked quietly. "The accident. He won't tell me."

Brennon took a deep breath and pulled his arm out from around me so he could run both hands down his face. "Steve was crazy," he said, only the words brought out a bit of a smile. "We were dormmates our freshman year at Stanford, and I knew right off the bat he was not someone who could live a small life. He's…he's smarter than he lets people think. It's not like he's manipulative, but he can read people and know exactly how to use their weaknesses to his advantage. Like, when he was a kid. He started his own business when he was twelve, delivering groceries to those who had a hard time getting to the store on a regular basis. He hired on a few other kids, and it quickly turned into a citywide thing.

"By eighteen, he had a couple hundred employees and a constant influx of cash without having to lift a finger. He had school paid for, excelled in all his classes, and every other weekend he was off on some adventure. Skydiving, cliff jumping, skiing in the Alps. He had his own racecar for a bit—not kidding—and by the time we graduated, he was being scouted by some of the top businesses around the world. Within a couple of years, he got hired on at one of the best tech companies in San Francisco, really high on the ladder for anyone let alone a twenty-four-year-old kid from Brooklyn who doesn't even have a background in tech. He even got engaged."

My stomach flipped—not that I'd been at all calm listening to what Brennon was saying—and I waited silently to hear how everything fell to pieces for the man who was just on the other side of a wall. Even though I wasn't sure I wanted to hear it. The Steve I had been getting to know was so different from the one Brennon was describing, and I knew that change had happened because of the accident, whatever it was. He had clearly lost more than just his eyesight, and my heart ached for him as I listened to Brennon's narrative.

"Steve was heading for greatness," he continued. "A couple years into the job he met Amelia—his fiancée—and they bought a house in Pacific Heights. He proposed, and they had their wedding planned in Cabo. He was in negotiations to become VP of the company when he was riding his motorcycle home and a truck ran a red light."

I grabbed Brennon's hand, though I wasn't sure which of us I was hoping to comfort. I could picture the accident too well, and suddenly it hurt to breathe as I imagined what that must have been like for Steve.

Brennon took another deep breath. "Thank God he was wearing a helmet," he said, "or he would have been dead. The impact broke his arm and collarbone, nearly shattered one of his ankles when he landed, but he hit his head. Hard. He was in a coma for four days, and none of us knew if he would ever wake up. When he did…"

"He couldn't see," I whispered. I thought getting passed over for promotions was bad, but that was nothing compared to this. This was waking up and realizing your whole life as you knew it was gone.

Nodding, Brennon wrapped his other hand around our entwined fingers. "Amelia stayed with him for a while, trying to help. But he wouldn't let her, and she left him about three months after the accident. He pushed everyone else away, and sometimes he wouldn't even let me in when I'd come to visit. Losing his sight… That took his whole life away from him. Everything he loved to do. Eventually, his company had to let him go because he didn't show up for work, and he pretty much had no reason to leave the house anymore.

"He basically disappeared after that, locked himself in his house and told me he was fine. Just recovering. But I went to visit him once after not hearing from him for a couple of days, and when he didn't answer the door, one of his neighbors said they hadn't seen him at the windows for a while or even any lights. I forced my way inside and found him…" He swallowed, and I wrapped my arm around his shoulders.

"I don't even know how long he'd been lying there," Brennan whispered. "Could have been a couple of days. He was literally starving. Unresponsive. The doctors told me he wouldn't have lasted much longer if I hadn't… My best friend nearly died because he couldn't even find the will to eat. He was in the hospital for a week, and then I brought him here. Took him to a therapist every week. He still stayed at home and rarely left the apartment, but for the last year, everything seemed good. Better. But if he's—"

"Hey," I said, both to stop him from talking about such horrible things and to protect him from falling into his own dark chasm. None of this was Brennon's fault. "He's fine. I promise. Practically devoured an entire smoked salmon today. You've been an incredible friend to him, and he knows that. Even if he doesn't say it."

Brennon's eyes held so much emotion that I almost couldn't keep eye contact with him. Gratitude and pain collided with an intensity that pulled at my chest and made me wonder if I could ever find anyone else who looked at me the way he was looking at me right then. When he leaned forward and kissed me, it felt like he was putting everything he couldn't say into his lips and his hands at my neck, and in that moment, I wondered if maybe I was wrong about never finding someone to love me.

"I am so glad I met you at that wedding, Lissa Montgomery," he whispered against my mouth, though I was almost too lost in his kiss to understand what he said.

And to think I'd almost left Seth's wedding early.

"Let's play a game," I said suddenly, sitting up straight as a wave of energy rushed over me. It had come out of nowhere, but I latched onto it. With Brennon gone all day at work, I didn't get many moments alone with him, and I was going to use this time to my advantage. "And before you try the excuse that you don't have any games," I added, "I know you do."

Grinning, Brennon pushed a curl behind my ear. He clearly appreciated the lighter mood, as sudden as it might have been. "Have you been rummaging through my stuff?" he asked.

"Without shame," I replied. "I had to know what sort of man you were before I stuck around for too long."

He teased another kiss against my lips, determined to throw me off. But this was a battle I would win. Likely realizing this, he sighed and sat up as well. "And what sort of man am I?"

"That depends."

"On what?"

"On how you play Monopoly."

He frowned. "Monopoly," he repeated. "You don't think I deal with enough money problems at work?" But his eyes lit up, which meant he was probably intrigued by the idea.

My mom and I had had plenty of crazy games when I was growing up, and I almost always managed to beat her. Soundly. It drove me to pursue a career in finance, and in the last decade, I had yet to be beaten by anyone. "I should warn you," I said, "I'm really good at Monopoly."

Narrowing his eyes, he slowly got to his feet and headed for the closet where he kept his games. "I thought you were supposed to be convincing me to play," he said. "Not cautioning me."

"You don't have a choice, so it doesn't matter."

"I had no idea you had such a competitive streak in you, Lissa."

I brought over the rest of the food and quickly helped Brennon set up the board and distribute the pieces on the coffee table. "This is why we have to play," I told him and chose the dog playing piece as I settled on the floor. "There's so much we don't know about each other, and Monopoly will bring all the dirty little secret personality quirks to the surface."

Brennon placed the top hat piece next to mine. A smile played at his lips, and he shook his head a little before he said, "If you end up forcing me to mortgage all of my properties, will you be a merciful lienholder?"

I gave him my very best wicked grin and replied, "That's for you to find out, my good sir. Roll the dice."

Brennon was not a yeller. He wasn't even a beggar. Though he barely had any money and had only a couple of useful properties left to his name, he sat on the floor opposite me and kept his eye contact firm and stoic. I had a full board of hotels and complete monopoly of the utilities, but I still hadn't broken him. I was impressed, and I couldn't remember the last time I had played against someone with quite this level of dignity.

"What's your move, Ashworth?" I asked, my voice low.

Brennon's mouth twitched as he sat there with the dice in his hands, just a few squares away from a rather large pool of money in the free parking. The odds of him rolling low enough were slim, but he had a chance to redeem himself if he rolled well. "You seem to think you can predict the future, Montgomery," he replied. "This isn't over yet."

"It will be as soon as you toss those dice."

Rolling the cubes between his hands, he examined the board as if searching for some way to bring himself back from the brink of extinction. It may have been two in the morning, but that hadn't stopped him from trying his very best to keep himself in the game. He was determined, and I very much liked that aspect of him.

"Here's the thing," he said.

"Just roll the dice!" I snapped.

Brennon smiled as if he'd just figured out some secret, and a bit of fear sparked into my chest. At this point I should have had the game in the bag, but he seemed to think it wasn't quite over. Though how he thought he could win, I had no idea. He didn't have any hotels. He barely had any houses on his properties. Without a way to shift the wealth from me to him, there was no way he could win, and yet his grin just kept growing.

"What?" I asked.

He chuckled a little. "You like to win, don't you?"

Obviously. "No one likes to lose, Brennon."

"But you like to *win*. Like, you like it a lot."

"So?"

He tossed the dice across the table, rolling an eleven and putting himself way past free parking. "It's just a fun little insight. A dirty little secret personality trait, as you said."

Cocking my head, I tried to figure out exactly what his smile meant. "Is it a good thing or a bad thing?"

As he moved his piece along the tiles on the board, Brennon kept smiling, and he hummed a little to himself, some punk rock song I had known in junior high. He landed on one of my hotels and clearly didn't have enough money to pay the rent, but he just grinned there like an idiot as he looked over his resources. "Looks like I need to give up," he said, tipping his hat over as if conceding defeat in chess.

"Then why are you smiling?"

He shrugged. "Because I like getting to know you."

That was adorable, but, "You're telling me you're perfectly okay with losing?" I asked. It would mean he was even better than I'd already discovered, but it was hard to believe he didn't care even a little that I beat him so completely. It was almost suspicious.

Brennon laughed, shaking his head as he rose to his feet. He offered me his hand, and then he pulled me straight into his arms as soon as I was up. "I mean, I would have liked to win," he said, and he spoke almost directly into my ear, sending shivers through me. "I'm not a robot. But that doesn't mean I won't spend every second I can with you just on the off chance you might get a reason to gloat for a while."

I rested my head against his shoulder, perfectly content to just stand there even though I knew I should make him go to bed so he wasn't dead in the morning. But knowing what I should do didn't change what I wanted to do, and the ball of warmth in my chest dictated my actions. "You sure know how to make a girl feel special," I said and lifted my head to kiss him.

He responded easily, pulling me closer. "Only the special ones," he murmured against my mouth.

It was probably the best goodnight kiss I'd ever had.

CHAPTER TEN

I woke to a gentle touch on my forehead and opened my eyes to find Brennon just a few inches away, a half-smile on his lips as he looked down at me in the dim light coming from the hallway.

"Sorry," he said. "I couldn't resist."

Goodness, he was handsome. It didn't matter what time of day it was; he always looked so put together and clean-cut and all around pretty. How did he manage to look so good after getting so little sleep, and on a couch no less? "You *should* apologize," I said, and then I grabbed him by the collar and pulled him down for a real kiss. "If you're going to kiss me, you might as well do it properly."

Grinning, he kissed me again then moved over to the closet to finish getting ready. At the moment, he was only in his boxers and his button-up shirt, and I watched him with a smile and wondered where I would have been right now if he hadn't approached me at Seth's wedding. Probably serving up pie at the old-fashioned diner down the street from my apartment because I badly needed a job and finding a new career wasn't going to be easy.

"Do you really have to go into the office so early?" I asked as I slowly sat up and leaned against the headboard. Seeing him for a few minutes in the mornings and an hour or two at night definitely wasn't enough for me. Especially after last night. "Just take a sick day."

He glanced back at me as he tucked his shirt into his pants, and I could see his resolve waver for a moment. I probably looked a mess, since I'd only just woken up, but he didn't seem to mind. "I haven't taken a sick day in nine years," he said, and then he began searching through his expansive collection of ties, humming softly as he did.

There were a lot of things I really liked about Brennon Ashworth. He was sweet, and thoughtful, and deliciously good-looking, and every new thing I learned about him seemed to add to his list of excellent qualities. But being a workaholic was not one of them, and I was starting to realize why Seth didn't like how much I worked. Was I as bad as Brennon?

I would have to try a little harder to persuade him. Slipping off his bed, I came up behind him and slid my arms around his waist. He stopped his tie search immediately, and I twisted around to his other side and slid my hands up to his neck. "You do feel a little feverish," I said sweetly.

He grinned and touched his forehead to mine, closing his eyes as he breathed me in. "I wish I could stay," he said and brushed his mouth against my lips. But apparently he didn't wish it hard enough, because in the next moment he reached behind me and grabbed a light blue tie.

I stepped back in disappointment. I thought about asking him if he would at least get home at a decent time, but I held my tongue. It wasn't like we were officially dating, and it wasn't like I didn't have anything else to do. I still had to make sure Steve was eating properly, and I had my future to plan out. No big deal.

At least Brennon sighed and looked appropriately sorry. "This project is important," he said, though he didn't seem thrilled with his own choice of excuse. "If there was any way I could..." Holding his tie up near my face, he studied me and the fabric for a moment then nodded. "Close enough," he said before wrapping it around his neck and tying it with the ease of someone who had been wearing ties every day for a long time. Had he always worked this hard? Something told me he had, and there was a high chance that wouldn't change.

Fully dressed now, Brennon kissed me on the cheek and gave me a winning smile that carried a hint of chagrin as he headed for the door with a quick, "See you tonight."

And as I stood there wondering what my best course of action was, I reminded myself that it was a bad idea to get attached to this man who didn't believe in love. I worried, though, that it was already too late, and I was quickly heading down a path that would lead me straight to heartbreak. I was smarter than this, and I knew it, and when I heard

Steve head into the bathroom and close the door, I squared my shoulders and took a deep breath.

Maybe things with Brennon weren't going to go anywhere, but that was fine. I'd known from the moment I met him that there likely wasn't any sort of romantic future with the guy. Besides, my reason for being here for the next few days instead of going back to Boston was on the other side of that wall, and I would see to it that Steve got back on track to living a full life. He deserved good things after what had happened to him, but he couldn't find those things on his own.

I had a job to do. If Brennon was going to be a workaholic, I might as well be one too.

How had the man gotten my number? I left my phone sitting on the counter in front of me as I whisked up some eggs to make omelets, and the words of the text I'd gotten a few minutes ago seemed to scream at me from the screen. I'd done really well staying fairly incognito, especially considering how many people tried to learn all my secrets when I was "dating" Seth. My personal phone number wasn't listed on any websites or directories—thank goodness for company phones—and I only gave it out to people I trusted.

So how had my father found me?

"I think you may be taking out a little too much anger on those eggs," Steve said carefully.

I looked up in surprise and gently set the bowl on the counter before I whisked the eggs into oblivion. I switched to chopping up veggies instead, the knife tight in my hand.

"Are you sure that's safer?" Steve asked.

"You don't even know what I'm doing," I argued, though maybe he was right. I came a little too close to adding some of my skin to the mushrooms.

"Some days are better," he said. He came around to my side of the counter and grabbed my hand before I murdered my own fingers. "Let me," he added and pulled the knife out of my hand.

Something was different, and I stared at him for at least thirty seconds before I figured out why he didn't look like himself. "You shaved," I realized out loud.

He kept one finger of his left hand on the blade of the knife as he cut with his right, therefore eliminating the risk of injuring himself as he slowly sliced the peppers, but even then he had to concentrate and therefore didn't respond to my comment until he'd finished the first half of a pepper. "I shaved," he repeated. "Oddly enough, people do that sometimes."

Given the length of his beard, it had been a long time since he'd done it last. Months at least, but probably longer. "Why?" I asked.

There was that bright smile again, only this time I could actually see it now that it wasn't hidden. I could see his dimples as well as the fact that he had a surprisingly soft jawline. Less of the male model features I'd expected and more of the "bring him home to meet your mother" sort of vibe. It really worked for him, even if his curly hair was a bit long. Had he always been this handsome?

"I wanted a change," he replied. "You don't have to cook every single meal for me, you know."

I kind of did, if I wanted to make sure he ate, but he didn't need to know that. Besides, "I happen to like cooking," I said with a grin.

Steve laughed. *Laughed.* Even the morning after the wedding, he hadn't managed it believably, but this sounded absolutely genuine. And it was a magical sound, like the sound of a man slowly coming back to life. "You happen to like a lot of things," he said and bumped his shoulder into mine.

I had no idea how to process everything happening this morning. I was already exhausted, and it was barely eight o'clock. "Well, someone should like them," I muttered, and then my eyes fell back on my phone where the text still sat waiting.

I heard you're still in California, it said. *Will you have dinner with me when I'm there at the end of the week?*

"Something wrong?"

I looked back at Steve and shook my head, only remembering he probably couldn't see it when his expression didn't change. "I'm fine," I breathed. *Wow, even I don't believe me.* "My dad texted me, is all." *Dad.* There were so many things wrong with that word.

Though he reached for the frying pan and set it on the stove, Steve frowned and kept his gaze toward me. "Most people consider that a good thing," he said softly. "I'd give anything to talk to my dad again."

Well that was its own can of worms, and I latched onto it immediately, hoping to steer the conversation away from me. "What happened to him?" I asked, though I was a little afraid it would ruin his cheery mood.

But Steve just kept working, carefully lighting the stove and grabbing a spatula in preparation. "He got sick when I was fifteen," he said, the words coming out a lot easier than I would have expected. "Luckily I got some time with him before he went, but it's never enough."

"And your mom?"

"Retired in Florida. She'll call every once in a while to check up on her baby boy."

I wondered if she knew how close she'd come to losing her baby boy. She probably didn't, or she would have called him every day just to make sure he was still alive. I silently praised Brennon for having the decency to keep her in the dark about that particular aspect of Steve's recovery, since I could imagine how difficult it would be for the woman to sleep if she knew.

"Now it's your turn," Steve said, folding his arms and turning to me. He was tall. I hadn't given it much notice before, but he had to have been at least six-foot-three, and I entertained the idea that even if I wore my highest heels, he would still be taller than me. That didn't happen often.

"My turn for what?" I asked.

"I'll start with the easy one," he replied, rolling his eyes. "How's your mom? The chef, right?"

I smiled. "She's great. Happily living with her husband in Vermont and working part-time in a little bed and breakfast."

"I'm assuming her husband is not your dad," he said, and he grabbed the butter and dropped a pat into the hot pan, rolling it around to get an even coat.

I didn't know how refreshing it would be to have someone who didn't know who I was related to. It was almost tempting to lie and make something up, but I had a feeling he would catch me in the act if I tried. Sighing, I glanced at my phone again then muttered, "Dear Dad is Gordon Hastings."

Steve dropped the pan, not quite making it all the way onto the stove, and it crashed to the floor, sending hot butter in all directions. He spit a curse, but luckily both of us had managed to avoid being scalded. "Sorry," he gasped, hurrying to find a towel or something.

I grabbed the pan before he stepped on it and tossed it into the sink, turning to stare at the man who furiously wiped at the floor in the hopes he got at least some of the butter splatter. Clumsiness was one thing, but that—I was pretty sure—had been complete shock. He only reinforced the idea when I heard him mutter, "How many kids does that man have?"

"You know Seth?" I asked hesitantly.

Steve slowly stood, twisting the towel in his hands. "Met him once or twice," he mumbled.

So that wasn't it. "Do you know my father?"

He shook his head and folded his arms. "Never met the guy."

Since Steve had already told me about his dad, there was only one option left. I knew Gordon Hastings wasn't the highest caliber of men, and there were rumors that Seth and I weren't his only children, but I'd never really put a lot of stock into the tabloids. Seth, however, was convinced there were others, and he'd spent a decent amount of time and effort trying to find them. He said he felt bad being the sole heir to a fortune when he had simply had a mother persistent enough to get Gordon to accept him as his son. His search hadn't been successful yet, but he knew it was only a matter of time before he uncovered another half-sibling.

So Steve must have known—probably well—one of these lost children, and that made things a little too real.

"We should go out," Steve said suddenly, tossing the towel into the sink and putting on a horribly fake smile. "I ruined breakfast, so we should go out and find something else. I know a great bakery not far from here."

A frying pan on the floor wasn't exactly ruining breakfast, but I had no intention of stopping Steve from willingly leaving the house. I doubted it could be very thrilling, being stuck in an apartment day after day. Fresh air would do us both some good. "A bakery," I said and decided I was glad for the change of subject too. He didn't need to know about my father still trying to connect with me, and I *really* didn't need to know the answer to who my potential sibling was. For now, Seth was the only one I had the energy to know about. "That sounds delicious."

"Perfect," Steve said, heading for the door. "You drive."

Luckily for us, choosing to go out for a late breakfast on a weekday meant the bakery wasn't absolutely packed with people, so when we sat at a table in the corner, we could actually hear ourselves think. The whole drive over, I had worried about how loud it might be and how distracting that probably was for someone who relied on his ears more than most, but I could breathe easy as we sat there.

Steve seemed to realize that too, his shoulders relaxing as soon as he was in his chair. Though maybe that was because he had a harder time navigating in an unfamiliar place and was just glad he didn't have to run into any more tables.

"Did you come here a lot?" I asked him as I glanced over the menu. Everything on it sounded incredible, and I could almost picture Steve showing up every morning for his daily bagel and smear. The chic little bakery certainly seemed like the sort of place an up-and-coming professional would frequent, much like Indie's coffee shop.

But he shook his head, frowning a little as he tried to read the menu. "I always wanted to," he said, "but I never had the time. What does..." His frown deepened. "I can't read it today," he muttered and held it out to me.

I quickly read out loud the menu then ordered for him when our server came to our table, and the whole time he sat slumped in his chair with his scowl firmly in place. I wished I knew how to help him keep that happiness on his own, because I wasn't going to be around forever. Brennon had his job and clearly cared more about work than relationships, and unless someone fell in love with the guy or we shipped him off to Florida, Steve was going to be on his own for the rest of his life. He wouldn't have someone looking out for him and helping him see the reasons to keep smiling, and I felt sick just thinking about the danger he'd be in.

"Something's wrong," he said suddenly, lifting his eyes to me and sitting up a little straighter.

My heart picked up a bit faster. "What?" I asked, pulling my phone from my pocket just in case.

The corner of his mouth twitched, hinting at a smile. "Not with me," he said and rolled his eyes. "With you. What's wrong?"

He wasn't quite right, but how did he know? "Nothing's wrong," I said.

"Something is," he insisted. "You're not usually this quiet. I'm waiting for the inquisition, but I keep wondering if you're still sitting there."

"Sorry?" I said, not sure what he meant by that last bit. I didn't think he liked my questions, so I figured he would rather have me silent instead of making his life difficult and annoying.

His smile grew a little bigger. "I mean, sometimes you're not exactly tactful, but it's kinda nice having someone to talk to."

That was good. Not wanting to be alone was a good sign, and maybe he wouldn't be completely hopeless when I was gone. "I'll try to be better," I told him. "I just have a lot on my mind today."

"Like what?"

"Oh, so it's my turn for the inquisition again?"

He nodded emphatically. "Does it have to do with your dad?"

Shrugging, I practically felt my phone burning in my hand with the unanswered message. "That's part of it. Not something I *want* to be thinking about right now, though."

"What else?"

I had no idea the man could be so persistent. I wasn't about to tell him I was thinking about him, so I reluctantly kept the subject focused on me. "The future, I guess."

"I was wondering about that, actually." He paused while our server put our plates in front of us—a terrible place to pause as my curiosity quickly filled in the rest with ridiculous notions, many of which involved Brennon—then he made a show of taking a large bite before he continued. At least he was smart enough to know I would make him eat if he didn't do it himself. "You live in Boston," he said, "but you came here for Catherine's wedding, right?"

"Right."

Two more bites. "That was several days ago, and I'm pretty sure you didn't plan to spend your little vacation with Brennon, since you hadn't met him before." The wrinkle appeared between his eyebrows as he softly added, "And I'm completely positive you didn't plan to spend your days stuck with a helpless, cranky blind man."

I would address his choice of adjectives in a moment, but first I had to reply, "What's your point?"

Setting his knife and fork down, he looked right at me, and for the first time I felt like he was really seeing me. "Why are you here, Lissa?"

Because most men in the world were imbeciles, and I was tired of fighting for a place at the table. "I quit my job," I said. "Last week."

"Why?"

"Eat your breakfast."

He scowled and shoved some eggs into his mouth. "Why did you quit?" he asked again before he'd even finished chewing.

What answer could I give that didn't end with me insulting his entire gender? "I realized I didn't want to waste my life making rich people richer." *Huh.* That sounded pretty good, actually.

"You were in finance?"

"An analyst," I confirmed.

"So now you're here because you have nothing better to do?" He almost looked disappointed about that, and my heart ached a little for the guy.

For the last two years, he'd managed to get rid of nearly everyone who cared about him, but he still craved companionship. Brennon wasn't around enough, and I was pretty sure Steve was simply lonely. If his fiancée had stuck around, been patient as he tried to adjust to his darker life, maybe he wouldn't have stopped eating. Maybe he could have figured out a way to keep working, and he could have kept his fancy house and lived his fancy life and actually enjoyed his existence.

I was starting to understand what his life felt like. Yes, I could see, and I could take care of myself—at least until my savings ran out—but my life had no purpose. I had nothing driving me. And if I kept up this way for too long once Steve no longer needed me, I would likely fall into the same metaphorical darkness that he had.

"You're thinking too hard again," he said quietly, reaching across the table and setting his hand on my arm (after missing it the first time). "How can I help?"

I sighed. "I stayed in California because I don't have anything to go back to," I told him. "My family is here, so I thought maybe it would be good to get to know my brother and his wife better. I'm *here*, specifically, because Brennon is worried about you and I offered to help. It's not that I don't have anything better to do. I'm here because I want to be."

Did he just blush? Coughing, he pulled his arm back, nearly knocking over his water but catching it before it drowned his waffle. "If you weren't here with me," he asked slowly, "what would you be doing with your time?"

"Honestly?" I thought for a second. "I have no idea," I said. "Maybe look for a job, since I'll have to find a place to live once Catherine and Seth are back. I have no intention of staying with them in that apartment of theirs, no matter how big it is."

Whatever he was going to say stopped before it hit his tongue, and he swallowed as he chose something else. "Well, we should do that today," he said.

I raised an eyebrow. "Sorry?"

"Find you a job. At least get some leads. There's a lot going on in this city, so I'm sure we could find you something."

How uncommonly thoughtful. Either he had cracked and could no longer keep sitting around listening to books, or there was a lot I didn't know about Steve Evans. Or both. Maybe he was always willing to help the people around him, but he didn't have the means most of the time. Maybe he was just deathly bored. Maybe he was trying to get rid of me as fast as he could. I had no idea what his motivation was, but more so, I didn't know if I wanted to let him do it. I was here to help *him*, after all.

"I don't even know what I want to do," I admitted. "All I know is finance, and I want to be able to help people."

"Bank teller," he replied with a shrug. "Tax specialist. In-home accountant for a small business. This is San Francisco, Lissa. You have a world of possibilities right in front of you."

"What if I don't want to be in finance anymore?" I said. I had no idea if that was true, but I was extremely curious to see what his response might be.

"Then we'll walk around until you see something that interests you."

My eyes going wide, I stared at him and tried to figure out if he was joking. I didn't think he was. "Walk," I repeated. "Around San Francisco. Are you crazy? What about your knee?"

He just rolled his eyes, slipping on his overly large jacket in anticipation. "Well we can't drive, can we? Not when you're the one keeping an eye out for ideas. And I don't think you want me behind the wheel, for several reasons. My knee is fine. I've walked on worse, trust me."

This was a terrible idea, but I couldn't think of any good reason to say no. Maybe he was right. Maybe it was the best way to figure out my potential career path. And anything that kept Steve out of the house and actually *doing* something was a good thing.

CHAPTER ELEVEN

Brennon called around two, and though the last few hours had left me feeling even more lost than before, I perked up when I saw it was him. He might have worked a lot, but at least he didn't forget about me when he was gone. "Hey, beautiful," he said by way of greeting.

Heat filled my face, and I turned away from Steve just in case he could tell how red I was. "Hey yourself. I'm glad you called."

"Why is that?" Brennon asked, sounding particularly excited.

"I was wondering if you wanted to come out and meet Steve and me for a late lunch."

He was silent for long enough that I checked my screen to make sure the call hadn't dropped. "Where are you?" he finally asked.

"Where are we?" I repeated to Steve, who leaned against a railing looking over the water. He just shrugged, and I shook my head at the stupidity of my question. "Fisherman's Wharf, I think it's called. Steve said they have some great crab somewhere around here."

Silence again. "Fog Harbor was his favorite," Brennon said eventually. "How did you manage to get him to leave the house?"

I glanced at Steve again and took a few steps away so more of the crowd was between us and he wouldn't overhear. He'd been in a good mood since leaving the bakery, and I didn't want to ruin it by calling attention to the fact that he was acting out of character. "It was his idea actually," I told Brennon. "I think he might have realized a bit of sun and fresh air could be good for him."

"Or something like that," he replied. What was that supposed to mean? "I could come for a little bit, I guess. Fog Harbor is on the east end at Pier 39. I'll meet you there in twenty minutes." He hung up before I could even show some excitement at being able to see him before tonight.

Weird.

Picking my way through the throngs of tourists wandering the wharf, I put my hand on Steve's shoulder and felt him stiffen beneath me until he realized it was me. "Brennon's coming to have lunch with us," I told him. "It'd probably be good to get you off your knee for a bit."

He grunted and turned in the direction we needed to go, but he kept one hand on the wooden railing, his knuckles a bit white from holding on so tight.

Navigating the crowd was bad enough when I could see them. I could only imagine how overwhelming it must have been for him, especially when I realized he'd closed his eyes. He said movement was easier to see, but there was probably so much movement happening that he could hardly take it all in. Somehow, I had to get him from here to the other end of the wharf, and I had to do it without reinforcing his belief that he was helpless so I didn't run the risk of losing what little ground I'd gained with him. *Simple.*

I slipped my arm through his and pulled close to him, and before he could speak his confusion, I said, "You'd think I would get used to crowds like this, living in a big city, but I still get a little freaked out by this many people around me."

Very slowly, he released the railing, turning his eyes to me with that wrinkle out in full force between his eyebrows. Either that was his default expression, or he couldn't decide what to make of me. I confused men a lot, but it felt different with Steve, like he was actually trying to figure out what made me tick instead of dismissing me as one of the many unfathomable women out in the world. "You should see Shanghai," he said softly. "This is nothing compared to that."

And that was all it took. Together we started forward, and he let me steer him down the wharf without a word of complaint.

We found the right restaurant, got our seats, and five minutes later, Brennon showed up. Before I could get a word of greeting in, he bent down and pulled me into an almost desperate kiss. I was so caught off guard that I just fell into it, though I was sure everyone else in the crowded restaurant wasn't exactly thrilled by his display.

I broke away from him long before I wanted to, reeling from the thrill of it, and smiled at him. "Not that I'm complaining…" I whispered.

"I missed you," Brennon explained before scooting his chair close to mine and sitting down. He slid his hand over my leg just above my knee, and only then did he turn to Steve. "Hey, buddy. You're looking sharp."

Steve just grunted and lifted his menu up in front of his face. I doubted he could read it any better than the one this morning, but he didn't seem eager to ask for help again.

"So," Brennon continued, "what have you two been up to today?"

I waited to see if Steve would say anything. He didn't. "Steve was helping me find a job," I said. "I'm hoping to stay in the area for a little while, but I can't do that without income."

Brennon glanced between us. "On Fisherman's Wharf?" he asked, directing that question more to his roommate.

Dropping his menu, Steve rolled his eyes and muttered, "She doesn't know what she wants to do. We were just looking for ideas."

"On Fisherman's Wharf," Brennon repeated as if it was the most outlandish idea he'd ever heard.

A bit red, Steve reached to hide behind his menu again, so I laughed and said, "I kind of like the idea of making chocolate. Or maybe being a fry cook in a place like this. I'm not shutting down anything until I find the right thing."

Steve sat frozen, and though he kept his gaze on the table, I could almost feel his focus on me. And somehow, I knew that almost-smile was meant for me.

"You're too smart for something like that, Lissa," Brennon said, rubbing his thumb across my knee. I knew he meant it as a compliment, but his comment didn't sit well in my stomach. It was a little too close to him telling me what I could and couldn't do.

"It's not about finding something difficult," I replied. "I want what I do to mean something. To make people smile."

"She'd make an excellent fry cook," Steve offered quietly. "She's trained by a chef, after all."

Now it was my turn to go red.

"You cook?" Brennon asked, his eyebrows high. "I mean, I figured you could cook, but…"

If he would stop bringing home takeout, he would be able to judge for himself. "I'm really not that great," I said.

Then Steve choked on his water. "Sorry," he sputtered and gratefully took the napkin I handed to him.

Brennon took my hand and leaned close, as if he was about to share some deep secret. My heart pounded a little harder as his gaze dug deep into me. A girl could seriously get lost in those eyes, and he knew exactly how to draw me in and make me feel like nothing else existed but him. "You'll have to show me tonight," he said quietly, and heat spread through my face as his nose brushed mine. "Then I can prove you wrong."

"I'll have the Crab Louie," Steve said loudly, and we slipped apart while our server pretended he hadn't noticed us.

Brennon coughed and made a quick glance at the menu. "Pacific Sole," he said. "Lissa?"

If I could get my face to stop burning, maybe I could focus on what was happening. I didn't like public displays of affection. The Davenports weren't terrible, but they had pushed my limits at Catherine's wedding and reminded me why I couldn't see myself like them. In love. I wasn't like Matthew, who was aware of Indie even when she was on the other side of the room, or like Lanna who couldn't help but smile when Adam was nearby. Seth may have been my brother, but he felt no shame showing the world just how much he loved his wife. I didn't do that. Even when I had dated in the past, I didn't kiss my boyfriends in front of other people.

Yet somehow Brennon had nearly completely overwhelmed me in the middle of a restaurant, and a large part of me wanted him to do it again. What was wrong with me?

"Louie," I stammered as Brennon returned his hand to my knee. "Crab. That sounds good. Yeah." And then the second our server left the table, I turned to Brennon and growled, "You need to stop," though I couldn't keep myself from smiling, which sort of negated my point.

With a low chuckle, Brennon gave me a swift kiss then moved to an appropriate distance. *Thank goodness.* "Steve cooks too," Brennon said as if we had never gotten sidetracked.

Steve immediately knocked his fork to the floor. "No, I don't," he argued as he bent to try to grab it.

"Well you used to."

"You're remembering things."

Brennon shook his head and turned to me, though I could barely keep my focus off of Steve, who looked almost panicked as he sat there gripping his newly retrieved fork. "He even went to—"

"Bren," Steve interrupted loudly, "could you show me where the restroom is? Kinda urgent."

"Oh." Brennon sat up straight, confused by the question. Maybe he'd never heard Steve ask for help before. "Yeah, okay."

Both men stood, and to my surprise, Steve actually grabbed onto Brennon's arm as they made their way through the tables. So he could let Brennon guide him, but he had a problem with me doing it? I didn't like how much that hurt, but I was too distracted by the pair of them to really pay attention to that part. They walked stiffly, and it almost looked like they were having a whispered conversation as they went. Was Brennon trying to figure out why Steve was hiding something? Or was Steve trying to say something to Brennon about his PDA? I couldn't tell, and I didn't like not knowing. Men were a lot easier to deal with when I could read them.

And they thought *I* was confusing…

As I sat there waiting, trying to understand two people I really didn't know at all, my phone started to buzz. Automatically, I pulled it from my pocket and answered the call as I kept my eyes in the direction of the bathroom. "Hello?"

"Lissa?"

My blood ran cold when I recognized my father's voice, leaving me frozen in my chair. "Gordon," I whispered and silently cursed myself for not bothering to look at the number before I answered. Or at the very least pretending it was a wrong number. Curse these men distracting me and adding unnecessary stress to my life. "What do you want?"

"You didn't answer my text."

On purpose, Dad. Deep breath. "Text?" I asked.

"I know you got it, Lissa. Why won't you let me try?"

"I don't know," I said. "Because you denied I existed for twenty-eight years? That might have something to do with it." Why did he have to call? Why couldn't he have just given up like any normal man-whore and just left me alone?

"Lissa, please. I know what I was, and—"

"Seth didn't want me to know you," I interrupted. "As soon as he realized who I was, he went off about his terrible childhood thanks to you." Okay, so maybe he didn't go off. But he had said more than once how glad he was his father had never claimed any other children. True, it would have been nice to get some share of the man's ridiculous worth, but Seth was convinced the wealth and fame and constant drive to be perfect just weren't worth it. My brother had endured a lifetime of being Gordon Hastings's child, and he wanted to spare me and any others the feeling of not being good enough.

"I'm not that man anymore," Hastings argued. "What will it take for you to believe me?"

"Leave me alone," I replied and hung up.

Brennon and Steve returned a few minutes later, neither of them in a good mood, and we spent the rest of lunch in a tense silence.

I didn't have the energy to give Brennon a kiss goodbye. Luckily, he didn't seem to have the energy either, and he just pulled me in for an extended hug that only slightly lessened the tightness in my shoulders left by my father's phone call. "I'll see you tonight," he whispered in my ear, leaving a chill at the base of my neck, and then he was gone. As was the sun, which disappeared behind a layer of clouds that had rolled in during lunch. Even the sky was as gloomy as me.

Steve and I made it halfway down the pier before he spoke, his hands in the pocket of his sweatshirt and his eyes fixed firmly on the ground where he stepped. "You wanna talk about it?" he asked.

I shrugged. Then I looked at him in confusion. "Talk about what?"

Veering right, he held out a hand and proceeded slowly until he found the railing protecting us from the edge. Then he turned, leaning his back against it and folding his arms tight across his chest. "You tell me," he said. "I can practically feel your tension, like this wave of heat rolling off of you. It's awful."

Awful indeed. And though a small part of me still wanted to keep my family issues close and personal, I wasn't sure I could hold onto something like this without talking about it. And right now, Steve was the only one here. "My dad texted me today," I muttered, settling against the railing next to him.

"Right. Hastings. And you're not too thrilled about that."

Of course I wasn't. "Up until a few days ago, he flat out refused to even say my name in case someone used that as proof that I was his flesh and blood."

"Ouch."

"Understatement of the century."

"And you're sure you're one of his?"

Unfortunately. "Mom was smart enough—creepy enough—to save some of his hair she found after he left her. She did a DNA test when I was born, and voila. Irrefutable proof. I grew up knowing my own father was a scumbag who abandoned my mom and probably hated me, and it only got worse after I met Seth. Hastings learned about me from the tabloids when I was twenty and even held a press conference to state that I was not his daughter."

Steve whistled low, shaking his head as he processed this. "That's…that's awful, Lissa," he said. "No child should feel unwanted, let alone flat-out rejected. But—you're welcome to smack me if I'm being indelicate—I have to ask: tabloids?"

I definitely smacked him, whacking him on the shoulder and bringing out a burst of laughter that seemed to bring the sun back out with it. "Is that really important?" I asked. "I'm baring my soul here."

"Sorry," he said, sounding sincere. "You just don't seem like the sort to find herself featured in gossip."

"I'm taking that as a compliment."

"You should." He unfolded his arms, and his shoulder rested against mine as he leaned a little closer. "I've never been able to take those women seriously," he said, "and for most of my adult life they were all I seemed to know. It's refreshing to know there are people out there like you. People who are worth knowing."

How was I supposed to respond to that? Swallowing, I eased just a little bit away so we were no longer touching, since the connection was a bit too distracting, and then I explained before he could ask again: "After Seth and I discovered we were siblings, he took on the responsibility of protecting me and going everywhere with me. Someone who saw us—she recognized Seth, of course—was convinced I was some secret girlfriend and snapped a picture, and suddenly the whole world knew who I was."

"I didn't," Steve said softly.

"That's because as soon as someone figured out we were related, not dating, the whole world promptly forgot about me."

Steve coughed, though it almost sounded like a laugh. "And now Hastings is trying to be a doting father and worm his way into your life?"

"He called when you were in the bathroom," I replied.

Did he just tense up? "What did he say?" he asked. Whatever I expected him to do, it wasn't this. He sounded almost angry as he stared at the ground and kept his head tilted toward me, listening intently for my reply.

I sighed. "Just… Just the same as before. He wants me to believe he's changed, that he wants to be part of my life."

"And do you want him to be?"

Why did it matter? "Not particularly," I said. "I trust him about as far as I can throw him."

"You could block him from your number."

I could have. "That seems a little…extreme," I said. Just like Steve's reaction. "Are you okay?"

Unclenching his fists—whoa, he really was angry—he rolled his shoulders out a bit and took a deep breath. "Sorry," he muttered, running a hand through his long hair. "I think I… We should talk about something else. We could get back to your job hunting."

That sounded even more exhausting than it did this morning. "I don't know," I said. "We should probably get you home so you can give your leg a rest."

"My leg is—" He stopped himself and took another obviously painful deep breath before turning to face me, his dark eyes almost burning as he met my gaze. "I don't want to go home," he said, and his voice wavered. "Not yet. Please. I don't know if I can spend another day stuck in that place. Please."

I'd never seen him so vulnerable, and I had to fight back a tear that threatened to slip from my eye. There I was, mourning the fact that my own father was desperately trying to be there and support me as his child, and Steve had literally lost almost everything he knew. My own woes were nothing compared to his, and my crab churned in my stomach with the guilt of knowing I had no right to complain. Steve needed me right now as much as I needed something to do to keep my mind off my father.

"Let's keep walking," I said and slipped my arm through his, relieved when he relaxed at my touch.

CHAPTER TWELVE

Have to work late. Dinner tomorrow? Miss you!

I glanced at my phone just long enough to read Brennon's message before slipping it back into my purse, and I hoped Steve hadn't noticed the light. He probably had no clue what time it was, and I had no intention of filling him in.

I wouldn't have guessed Steve could have so much to say. I had only briefly mentioned something about Seth and Catherine being in Fiji, and he went off about whitewater rafting the Navua River. That turned into describing the Northern Lights in Iceland, which turned into fishing excursions in Alaska, which became free diving in Zanzibar. The man really had been everywhere, and though I expected him to get moody when he remembered he likely couldn't do any of those things again, he simply lit up. Became human again.

I wasn't sure how many miles we'd walked, and I certainly hadn't spent any time looking around for places to work, but I had no regrets about the afternoon. Not when Steve hadn't stopped smiling, even when I failed to steer him around a puddle and he ended up with one shoe soaking wet.

Night had settled in now, and though I knew we should have been heading back, it was hard to want to stop Steve's stories. His life had been so...full. He hadn't wasted any time, and he hadn't let his own doubts convince him not to try something. I couldn't even imagine the sudden shift he'd gone through after the accident, and I walked next to him, wondering how he'd managed to keep going for so long.

He was so much stronger than I'd guessed at first.

"What?" he asked suddenly, and I realized I'd been staring at him for a little too long.

"Nothing."

"Sure."

"You're just…different." And I really didn't need to point it out, but I couldn't help myself. It was like the man who walked arm in arm with me was someone I'd never met before.

He laughed softly. "You mean I'm not acting like a helpless, cranky blind man?"

"Something like that."

Shrugging, he tightened his arm in mine a little as the sky above us continued to get darker. "I dunno," he said. "I guess I feel different. Freer than I've felt in a long time."

I smiled. "I'm glad." I really was. Even if I was only going to be around him for a short while, I was glad I had been able to do at least a little bit to improve his life. Hopefully he wouldn't go backward from here when I was gone living my own life again.

"It's all your fault, you know," he said, making my smile even wider.

"I think what you meant to say was, 'Thank you, Lissa, for letting me be the big strong man so you could wander the city without fear of being murdered.' Or, you know, something like that."

His arm tightened even more. "Where are we, anyway?" he asked. "I lost track, like, this morning."

I searched for the nearest street sign then said, "9th Street? And Mission Street."

Forehead crinkling, he thought for a moment then nodded to our right. "That's east, right?"

"I'm impressed."

"The car should be over that way somewhere, assuming you haven't gotten us completely lost." He was tired, and I mentally smacked myself for not realizing it earlier. He could barely walk on his swollen knee, and he looked ready to fall asleep while standing as he struggled to keep his eyes open. Not that they were doing him much good in the dark anyway, but still.

"Getting sleepy on me?" I asked, trying to sound teasing instead of worried.

He grinned, but then he dropped his smile as he froze. "Did you hear that?"

Well that was a good way to make a girl freak out. "What?" I whispered, suddenly wishing I'd brought my pepper spray.

He held up a finger, leaning his head toward the alleyway to our right. "Listen," he whispered.

I did, but it wasn't so late that the sounds of the city had faded. All I could hear were cars and the chatter from a nearby restaurant. "Steve? What is it?"

Pulling away from my grip—he had to fight a little because I held so tight—he took a couple of wary steps into the alley. Then he crouched and held out one hand, his palm up, and clicked his tongue. "Hey there," he said gently.

An animal? I crouched next to him so I wouldn't be as intimidatingly tall. "Dog?" I whispered.

"I think so. Come here, buddy. It's okay."

I pulled my phone from my purse and turned on the flashlight, shining it into the alley. At first all I could see was garbage spilling from a dumpster, but then I caught sight of a mass of dirty fur shivering in the corner. "Oh no," I whispered and hurried forward.

The dog—I almost wasn't sure that was what it was because it was so dirty and matted—barely managed a whimper when I approached, its big brown eyes wide and terrified. I couldn't tell how thin it was through its fur, but I knew it was struggling, its little lungs pulsing way too fast. "Steve, come hold this for me."

He moved slowly through the darkness, but his fingers found my shoulder, and then he took the phone from my hands. "Is it hurt?" he asked, a slight tremor in his voice.

"I can't tell." I held my hand out, moving as slowly as I could so I didn't scare the thing. It lifted its head just enough to sniff my fingers, and then it whimpered again. "We're here to help you," I told the dog and cautiously rubbed its head between the ears. It leaned into my touch, and its tail lifted in a feeble wag. "That's right. We're your friends." Then I turned to Steve, my heart aching a little. "I don't think it can move," I told him.

Nodding, Steve thought for a moment then said, "Go get the car. I'll stay with it, maybe see if I can get it to stand up."

I went as fast as I could, both for the dog's sake and for Steve's. I didn't want to leave him alone in the dark any longer than I had to. By the time I got back to the alley, my heart was racing from adrenaline, and I found Steve leaning against the wall, the pup shivering in his arms. "How's it doing?" I asked softly to announce my return.

He kept focused on the dog, as if he was worried to break eye contact with it. "He needs help," he said.

Cupping my hand around his elbow, I led him to the car and opened the passenger door for him. "I'll see if I can find a vet or someone who's still open."

A quick search told me the only emergency vet was clear on the other side of the city. A quick glance at Steve as I climbed into the car told me he badly needed to get home where he could rest. He'd dropped his head back against the seat, his eyes closed as he cradled the dog, and the pair of them were an awful sight.

"We're taking him home," I decided out loud.

Forcing his eyes open, he turned to me in surprise and said, "We are? But—"

"We can bring him to a vet in the morning, but right now he needs some food and water. And a good bath."

"I don't know how Brennon will feel about—"

"Let me worry about Brennon," I said and shifted the car into gear. "You just worry about the dog." I drove as quickly as I could through the evening traffic, half my focus on the two creatures next to me as I thought about what I needed to do to help them both.

When we reached the apartment, I only had to get two steps ahead of Steve to realize he had paused just inside the door. When I glanced back, he blinked hard a couple of times then shook his head. "It's bad," he said, a waver in his voice. "When I'm tired, I can't…"

"We're almost there," I assured him and went back to slide my arm across his back so I could guide him. He practically shook from the effort of holding the dog, and I held onto him a little tighter. "Let me take him," I said.

"I'm fine."

"Steve."

"Just tell me where to go."

Silently groaning, I directed him to the bathroom and flipped on the light. As Steve gently set the dog in the tub, I hurried back to the kitchen and grabbed a package of sliced turkey. And then I paused in the front room, letting myself take a deep breath. This was a bad idea. For so many reasons, most of all because Steve was so exhausted. I was supposed to be looking after him to make sure he didn't worsen his injuries or damage his sight more, and here I was letting him carry a stray, possibly rabid dog into an apartment that wasn't even mine.

A week ago, I was staring down a man who couldn't care less about my job performance and cared only about himself and his image. Now I was facing a man who didn't seem to care about himself at all. This was new territory for me, and I nearly grabbed my phone and called Brennon to beg him to come help me, since he'd dealt with Steve at his worst and knew what to do.

"Don't be stupid, Lissa," I muttered and put my phone on the counter. I didn't need Brennon to do something I could handle on my own. Besides, I worried he would only make it worse.

Steve had turned the water on low and pulled the showerhead down, holding it close to the dog to keep the water from splashing too much. He murmured to the dog at the same time, too softly for me to hear what he said. But the dog had his eyes open wide and fixed on Steve as if he was life itself. Maybe he was.

"I brought some food," I said gently and put my hand on Steve's shoulder.

"I can't see what to do," he replied. And he sounded miserable about the fact.

"Take this," I said, holding the meat in front of him and grabbing the showerhead. "You're doing great, but maybe you can try to get him to eat something."

The poor dog was worse than I'd thought, the water barely making a dent in the dirt. It took twenty minutes of intense scrubbing before I could tell it was a young golden retriever beneath all the grime, but at least Steve had gotten it to swallow the meat. It perked up a little after that, still mainly focused on Steve aside from the occasional lick in my direction, but I had no way of knowing if it had any internal injuries or infections or parasites or anything it might have encountered out on the street. That was the hardest part, not knowing how to help it.

That, and not knowing how to convince Steve to let me take care of the dog so he could go to sleep.

"Don't say it," Steve said out of the blue.

I paused my scrubbing to stare at him. "What?"

Sighing, he closed his eyes but kept his focus on me. "You have a...feeling about you," he said.

Yes, that totally helped me understand what he meant. I turned off the water—the dog was about as clean as he'd get without professional help—and sat back against my feet where I knelt. "A feeling," I repeated.

"There's just this… I don't know, like a tension or… It's hard to explain."

"Clearly."

Grabbing a couple of towels from the little shelf across from the toilet, Steve handed one to me then draped the other over the dog. With a grunt, he rose to his feet, though he barely put any weight on his bad knee as he stood there. "You feel like Brennon does when he's extra worried about me," he said finally.

So the blind man had a sixth sense. *Awesome.* "I think there's a reason for that, buddy," I said. "You should go to bed."

He folded his arms, tilting his head a little to the side. "*You* should go to bed," he replied. "You know, I've never liked people telling me what to do."

"Neither have I," I said, and a smile played at my mouth though I had no idea why. I was too stressed out about this dog and this man and my father and Brennon and life in general to be smiling right now.

Steve broke into a smile too, only his was more of a lopsided smirk that made him way too attractive for a man who spent his days locked up alone in an apartment. "So what are we supposed to do now?" he asked. "Arm wrestle to decide who's going to bed and who's going to dry off Captain?"

I stood as well, though he had a good five inches on me and wouldn't likely be as intimidated by me as the cowards I used to work with. He couldn't see me anyway. "You think you could beat me in an arm wrestle?" I asked. "You weigh, like, a hundred pounds."

"Ouch." But his grin widened. "What about a battle of wits?"

That sounded more intriguing than it should have. "I'm pretty sure I would win that too," I said. "Hang on, did you just call the dog 'Captain'?"

"He needed a name."

"And why did you get to decide what it was?"

"I was the one who found him."

I narrowed my eyes. "You may have heard him," I said, "but *I* was the one who found him."

"I carried him to the car," he argued.

"I'm the one who just spent half an hour making him look human again. I mean dog. Doggy. Whatever."

Steve laughed, the sound echoing off the walls of the small bathroom. He had such an incredible laugh that it was distracting me from my argument, and I wanted to just stand there and listen to him laugh instead of standing my ground. "You're so weird," he said as the dog's tail thumped his approval of the man's happiness. I fully agreed with the dog.

"I still think I should get a say in the dog's name," I replied, my cheeks warm.

"Well what do you want to call him?"

Glancing at the dog, who rested his chin on the side of the tub as he watched us with big brown eyes, I stood there and wondered when the last time was that I'd been able to banter with someone like this. Seth was always fun to tease, but I didn't see him all that often when we lived on other ends of the country. And I didn't know Brennon well enough to know how to tease him.

I spent more time with his roommate than I did with the guy I was dating.

"I think it needs to be something brave," I said as that thought rolled around in my brain. Was that the reason Brennon gave me that overpowering kiss at lunch today? Because he was jealous Steve saw me more than he did? *Don't be stupid, Brennon.* He was the one who worked crazy hours instead of spending time with me. It certainly wasn't *my* fault.

"Definitely brave," Steve said. He crouched down and rubbed the towel over the dog's sopping fur.

I stooped down to help him. "And it should be strong," I said. "Confident."

"Absolutely," Steve replied.

"And heroic. He seems like a heroic dog."

"Can you really think of a name that fits all of that?" Steve asked, and his hand slipped on top of mine.

We both paused in our drying, and I looked up at him as he looked down at me, his eyes fixed on mine. Yet again I wondered how much he could see, or if I was just a shadow and a blur to him. When most men looked at me, they looked at me with interest. My brother was known around the country as one of the sexiest men alive—he threatened to toss me into the ocean when I brought that up once—and he definitely got most of that from our father, who obviously was handsome enough to have left a string of pregnant women all around the country. Catherine said I inherited the same good fortune as Seth had and even disliked me for a while because of it.

But the problem with generally being considered pretty was never knowing why people did the things they did. Did I get my analyst job because I was the most qualified? Or because Mikaelson liked my face the best? I never put a lot of effort into my appearance just because it shouldn't have mattered.

So why did it suddenly matter now?

"I think I have the perfect name," I whispered.

Steve leaned a little closer. "Do you now?"

I bit my lip to keep my grin from giving me away and let the silence drag on just a little longer than I should have. Building the suspense. "What about Captain?" I said.

His jaw dropped, incredulity in his eyes. "Lissa, you are…"

Laughing, I pulled my hand out from under his and carefully lifted the dog, pulling him against my chest even though he was still super wet. We needed to get him somewhere more comfortable, somewhere warmer. And I needed to get a little distance from Steve. "What am I?" I asked Steve as I stood.

"Impossible," he replied immediately. "You're impossible, is what you are. Where are you going?"

"The couch."

"Why?"

"So I can put on a movie while I keep trying to get my new friend dry."

"He's your friend, is he?" Putting his hand on my shoulder, Steve followed me out to the front room and onto the couch, where I set the dog between us and resumed my towel drying.

"I am the one who found him," I said.

"I'm the one who carried him," Steve replied.

"Just the first time. I carried him the second." I smiled, both because of the ridiculousness of our argument and because Captain immediately put his head on Steve's lap, pulling himself closer. "Okay," I said, "maybe he is your friend. Heaven knows you could use one."

"Meaning?" He frowned, a bit of an edge to his voice. *Poor guy.*

"Meaning you're friends with Brennon Ashworth," I replied and shifted a little closer to the dog so he'd be warmer. "So I'm not sure how good your taste really is."

Steve rolled his eyes and leaned in so he could rest his arm across

Captain's back and easily rub his neck. "Are you saying I made a bad choice in keeping Bren around?" he asked.

I'd forgotten how comfy Brennon's couch was, and I slid a little deeper into the cushion to rest my head against the back. I turned my face to Steve and gazed into his dark eyes as he gazed right back at me with that confused wrinkle on his forehead. "You could do better," I said.

"So could you," Steve replied.

I didn't know what to say to that, so I didn't say anything at all.

A soft sound woke me from my light sleep. I wasn't sure how long I'd been out, but I'd never gotten around to putting in a movie. Steve had zonked out pretty quickly, though I didn't remember his head falling onto my shoulder. What was it that woke me up?

Brennon.

He stood a few feet from the couch, his blue tie hanging untied around his neck and his jacket in one hand. Though it was dark, he looked right at us, taking the strange scene in with his eyebrows low. I didn't blame him, considering there was a real-life dog sleeping soundly on the couch with us.

Not wanting to wake Steve, who badly needed the sleep, I smiled at Brennon and hoped he understood how happy I was to see him.

Brennon didn't smile back. "I'm exhausted," he whispered, though he didn't need to say it out loud for me to guess as much. What sort of work had kept him at his office past eleven? "I'll see you in the morning," he added then shuffled off to his room, closing the door behind him.

"Looks like I get to share the couch," I whispered to myself. It wasn't the most comfortable position, but there was nothing that would make me move. I just gently rested my head against Steve's and closed my eyes, quickly falling back into a dreamless sleep.

CHAPTER THIRTEEN

Captain was potty trained. That was nice. A dog slobbering all over me at six in the morning because he needed to go out was less nice. "That's disgusting," I mumbled and held up my hands to protect myself from further drooling.

Steve snorted, still half-asleep on my shoulder. "There's my good boy," he said.

I shoved him away. "Do you have any rope or something so I can take him outside?" I asked.

Yawning wide, it took him several seconds to answer, "You're asking the wrong person," as he brushed his hand over his thick mess of hair. "You could try the closet," he added, limply waving toward the little closet near the front door.

Suddenly a different dog from last night, Captain stayed right on my heels as I hurried to the closet where I'd found cleaning supplies before and dug through a box on the floor. No rope, but I did find a roll of duct tape. Better than nothing. Tearing off a long strip, I quickly folded it in half the long way so all the sticky was hidden and kept working until it was long enough to act as a sort of temporary leash.

"Okay, bud," I said and looped my little tape rope around Captain's neck, just tight enough that he couldn't escape if he wasn't as trained as I was hoping. He immediately pulled toward the door, desperate to get outside.

We barely reached the sidewalk before Captain found the nearest weed growing in a crack and promptly popped a squat. "Good boy," I muttered, and only then did my exhaustion catch up to me as my adrenaline dissipated. Sleeping upright on a couch: not a good way to spend the night. My sleepiness settled on me like a fog to match the grey gloom that seemed to hang over the city every morning. Boston had its occasional fog, but it didn't quite compare to the Golden Gate's disappearing act every day.

And yet, despite the all-around gloominess of the morning, I was really starting to like this city. Maybe relocating here wouldn't be so terrible. As soon as I actually woke up, I would head upstairs and hop on my computer to do some real job hunting, since I hadn't gotten any closer to finding one yesterday.

Finished with his business, Captain planted himself right at my feet and looked up at me with big brown eyes that weirdly reminded me of Steve, though I seriously doubted the man could pull off the puppy-dog look. He was thin from being hungry, but for the most part this little dog seemed happy and healthy, and I stood there wondering if he had a home out there. I almost hoped he didn't. If I had to go inside and tell Steve he couldn't keep the dog...

The door to the apartment building slid open to let someone out, and I glanced over instinctively.

"Brennon!" I said, jumping a little in surprise. It was so early.

He paused just outside the door, fully dressed with his phone in his hand and his gaze hard. "Oh," he said.

Oh? That was it? "You're leaving already?"

Nodding, he glanced around then stepped a little closer. Was it just me, or was he actively avoiding the dog at my feet? He was acting so differently from the Brennon I thought I knew that it felt like I was looking at a mask instead of the real him. How many of those did he wear, I wondered. "I have to finish the project I was working on last night," he said. "I'm not sure how long it'll take."

My heart sank, but a bit of annoyance flared up in me too. Not at Brennon, but at myself. I knew it was a bad idea to let myself get so attached so quickly. I *knew* it. We barely knew each other, and I had no reason to expect him to drop everything just to spend his time with me. I should have figured that out yesterday when I tried to convince him to stay home. "Of course," I said. So much for being smart and responsible.

Finally, Brennon let his eyes drop to the pup, and though he frowned, he nodded a little. "Steve needs something like this," he said softly. "Someone to keep him company after you're..."

I didn't like the sound of that. "Maybe," I said carefully, "I can, uh, bring by some dinner later. If you're still stuck at the office. If it wouldn't be too distracting." In the past, I fought against being clingy, but apparently I hadn't successfully managed to get rid of that trait completely. I felt like I was begging him to let me be part of his life, and I knew that would not end well. He had been up front with how he felt about love, and I had to remember that.

But he smiled, gave me a swift kiss on the cheek, and muttered, "I'll try not to be too late," before he hurried off to catch the bus.

While I had my suspicions of why things were so weird between us, I forced down whatever conclusions my brain was jumping to and told myself Brennon was just stressed and busy. It had nothing to do with Steve because there was no reason for it to have anything to do with Steve. He was becoming a good friend, nothing more, and in a few more days, he wouldn't need me to hang around. We could all get back to normal life, whatever that might look like for me.

"Let's go back inside, buddy," I said, giving Captain a gentle tug for him to follow me back to the elevator.

As soon as I opened the apartment door, Captain pulled hard enough on the rope that it slipped from my fingers, giving him the freedom to hurry back to the couch and jump up onto Steve's legs as he lay there.

"Did you just make a leash out of duct tape?" Steve said almost immediately.

Rolling my eyes, I headed for the kitchen to start making some breakfast for both the boys. More deli meat for Captain, and sausage and eggs for Steve. "Are you jealous of my ingenuity?" I asked.

He chuckled, his fingers rubbing between the dog's ears once he removed the rope from his neck. "A little bit terrified of it, maybe."

"You don't have to be jealous. Not everyone can be as astonishingly bright as me."

"Right."

Instead of arguing—we would go on forever if I tried—I turned my focus to breakfast while Steve chatted softly with the dog. I couldn't help but think about what would happen to Steve once I found my own place and left. Would he actually keep Captain? If the dog already had a home, someone missing him, would he find himself a different dog? It didn't have to be a trained guide dog, and Steve had changed a lot over the last few days. I knew I couldn't take credit for all of it, but surely I'd made some good progress with him. I just hoped he wouldn't revert back to his mopey self the second I stepped out that door.

"Any word from your father?" Steve asked.

I hadn't charged my phone since yesterday, but I really had no desire to plug it in and check. "Not today," I replied and cracked an egg onto the hot skillet. Brennon didn't even know my father had tried to talk to me after the wedding. I wondered if he would have asked about it if he did.

"It was Amelia," Steve said.

I froze just as I was about to crack another egg. "What?"

"My fiancée," he said. I couldn't bring myself to turn toward him as he spoke, so I had no idea if he was watching me as he continued, "Amelia. She didn't know her dad wasn't really her dad, but after my accident, her mom told her... She was a Hastings. Like you. And her mom wondered if maybe Gordon would be willing to help his daughter's fiancé. Not that I needed him to. But that's why I sorta...freaked out. Or whatever. You just don't expect to meet a lot of people who could be related like that, you know?"

I wasn't completely sure how to handle this information, and I stood there with a spatula in hand and my thoughts swimming around and making me dizzy. Apparently I still wasn't completely awake. "I should..." I swallowed. "I should tell Seth about her," I said. "He'd be able to find out if she's really..." What if I had a sister? An honest to goodness half-sister who once upon a time was in love with the man just a few yards away from me. If Seth found her, then what? Would we adopt her into our makeshift family and have little get-togethers to commiserate over the grief of having a man like Gordon Hastings for a father?

I could tell her about Steve. Maybe, if she knew he was better, she would want to get back with him. He wouldn't have to be alone anymore.

"She got married about six months ago," Steve said quietly.

This time I did turn, but he hadn't moved from where he lay, even though Captain had practically stretched out across his whole chest.

"Brennon tried to keep it from me," he continued, "but I heard him on the phone with my mom. He was worried I would..."

I swallowed again. "How do you want your eggs?" I asked.

Turning his head, he searched the void of his sight for a glimpse of me with his dark eyes. The little wrinkle between his eyebrows came out in full force, and he gently nudged Captain to make him move. He winced as the dog's paw dug into his stomach—wince was an understatement—and moved slowly as he sat up. Too slowly. And he was paler than usual.

My heart pounded faster. "Steve, what's wrong?"

He shook his head but closed his eyes, choosing to sit there at the edge of the couch instead of standing, like I was sure he planned to do. "I'm fine," he muttered.

"What's wrong?" I repeated.

Using the couch's armrest to push himself up, he gingerly shuffled his feet across the floor as he made his way toward me, grabbing the back of to his feet one of the kitchen chairs as soon as he was close enough. "You're too paranoid," he said as he lowered himself into the chair. "I'm just a little sore from yesterday. Promise."

Maybe that made sense. "You're sure?" I asked.

He smiled, and that was enough to convince me. The man didn't smile easily. "Do you really think I would lie about something like this?"

"I don't even know you," I replied. *Stop talking.* "Are you the sort of person who lies?" *Seriously, Lissa, wake up and realize you need to stop.*

Steve's eyes somehow managed to lock onto mine, and my heart tremored in my chest. "I would never lie to you, Lissa."

"I believe you," I said.

"Sunny side up," he replied, and his grin cleared the rest of the fog from my head.

"This is the most adorable dog I have ever seen." Indie had nearly dropped a pot of coffee in excitement when she saw us outside her shop, so I definitely believed her. Especially because she'd been sprawled on the sidewalk with her fingers in Captain's fur for the last several minutes. "Where did you get him?"

I wasn't sure why I suggested we stop for coffee. Steve and I had spent the morning making sure everything was good with Captain. He had no microchip, and no one had posted anything about a missing Golden. The vet said he was surprisingly free from parasites and up to date on his shots, and aside from a bit of malnutrition, he was right as rain. We stopped at a pet store and picked up all the essentials—Steve insisted on choosing the collar, even though he could hardly tell one from the next, and picked a light blue—and we were on our way back to the apartment when I recognized the street and asked if Steve was interested in some coffee.

He hadn't even hesitated in saying yes.

"We found him," I said, giving Indie a smile.

"He found us," Steve corrected from where he sat with Matthew at one of the outside tables.

I had no idea why it mattered so much, but I was glad Matthew seemed content to talk with my new friend while Steve drank his coffee. Steve needed friends in this city as much as I did, and I doubted there could be anyone better than the Davenport family. From the little I knew about Matthew, his lighthearted nature and inherent kindness was exactly what Steve needed.

"Are you keeping him then?" Indie asked me.

That was a harder question to answer than I realized. "Steve is keeping him," I said, "though I'm claiming partial custody. You know, every other weekend and whatnot."

Indie laughed, and Captain responded to her happiness with a matching wag of his tail and a kiss on her chin. "Oh, aren't you just the sweetest little thing? So." Her voice dropped into a whisper, her eyes alight with mischief. *Uh oh.* "Tell me about this Steve guy."

This Steve guy had better than average hearing and had to have heard her question. Grabbing her hand—I knew better than to think she would let me change the subject—I pulled her inside the coffee shop and far from the open door. "Don't look at me like that," I said, shaking my head. "He's just a friend."

"So why are we in here?" she asked.

"Because I don't want him to hear us."

"Why not? A man probably wants to know exactly what a beautiful girl thinks about him."

"I'm dating his roommate," I said. At least, I was pretty sure I still was. I hadn't heard from Brennon yet, though my phone *was* clinging to the little bit of charge I'd given it before we left the house and was probably too low on battery to get any calls or texts. I sipped on my coffee as I silently told myself not to jump to conclusions where Brennon was concerned. He worked hard, and he was probably too busy to grab his phone. He would call at lunchtime, like he had every day.

Indie cocked her head. "Does *he* know you're dating his roommate?" she asked, nodding toward Steve.

I choked. "What? Steve?"

I really didn't like the look of her grin as she watched me try to breathe again. "Sure," she replied. "I know he can't see, but that hasn't stopped that man from looking over at you every thirty seconds since you got here."

"He's probably just making sure I haven't left him to fend for himself," I said, turning just in time to meet Steve's gaze through the window, so to speak. Why would he keep looking at me?

Still grinning, Indie waited a moment then asked, "So who's this roommate? When did you meet him?"

"At the wedding," I said. Steve was still looking pale, though he hadn't seemed too bothered by whatever soreness he had when we were walking around the pet store. I hoped he was okay, but it was hard to tell. He barely moved as he sat there.

"That's not very long," Indie said. "Is it serious?"

Good question. "I dunno," I muttered. Steve would tell me if he was in pain, wouldn't he? I didn't want to think that he actually was capable of lying to cover up a problem, and I really did believe him when he said he wouldn't lie to me. I desperately wanted to believe him. "Brennon doesn't believe in love," I said slowly, "so it's hard to know if there's a future there."

"Doesn't believe in love? What kind of bull—crap—is that?" A bit red, Indie glanced at the customers around us, probably hoping no one had heard her. "Wow, I've been spending too much time around Matthew and Catherine, sorry."

I just smiled. I really did like Indie, and I hoped Matthew wouldn't screw things up with her. She belonged in this family. "He says he thinks it's just fantasy," I replied. "Romantic nonsense made up by people hoping there's a magical solution to life's problems. Love is just contentment. Compatibility. Safety."

"Well yeah," Indie said, rolling her eyes. "Everyone knows that, but they don't have any problem calling it love. What does Brennon have against the word?"

Steve looked over at me again, searching me out among the shapes and colors of the coffee shop. Why would he be looking for me when he had Captain by his side? "I have no idea," I muttered.

Indie took my hand, and I stared at it for a second before looking up into her face. With her black hair, green eyes, and a splash of freckles on her nose, she had a bright sort of kindness about her, a fire that made her absolutely stunning in her own unique way. Matthew probably fell for her the second he saw her.

"Did you know I was married?" Indie asked quietly. I shook my head. "For a few years, and I thought I knew what love was. How could I not, when my husband looked at me the way he did and made me want to be something better? After I lost him, I understood love even more. It was caring more about someone else than about yourself, and being willing to give up everything for just one more minute with them. And then I met Matthew."

Her smile said a lot more than words could when she looked out at him through the open door. As if he knew she was watching him, he looked over and mirrored her expression before returning his attention to whatever Steve was saying to him. Anyone who saw them would have to admit the two of them were nothing if not made for each other. "When I met Matthew," Indie continued, "I realized love is different. Every day. It's sharing your fears and letting someone take some of your burden for a bit. It's letting yourself be real. A man who says he doesn't believe in love is a man who's afraid to let his guard down enough to feel vulnerable."

I knew it was a warning, an admonition to stop me from getting hurt, but I wasn't sure how much I wanted to hear it. I knew love was real and that it was different for everyone. I could see that just in Matthew's family alone. But she was telling this to someone who didn't need to hear it. "You don't have to worry about me," I said quietly as the morning's fog returned, settling heavy in my chest. "I doubt anyone will be falling in love with me any time soon. Not the real me, anyway."

Her smile warm, Indie pulled me in for a hug. "I know I really don't have a right to say this," she said, "since we met less than a week ago, but I think you're wrong. Love likes to sneak up on you when you least expect it. Like when it walks through your door and turns your life on its head."

Like when you meet a charming guy at a wedding on the other side of the country. "I should get Steve home," I muttered, slipping out of her embrace. "Thanks for talking to me."

"Don't forget to see what's right in front of you," Indie said then led the way back outside.

Steve and Captain both perked up as we approached, and my stomach twisted a little. Indie was in my head now, and I couldn't help but wonder if her hints weren't just hopeful thinking on her part. Was there more to Steve's little glances than I thought?

"You ready to go?" I asked, touching his shoulder. "I've got a plan for lunch I think you might like."

Why was Matthew grinning like that?

"Actually," Steve said, "I was hoping you'd let me do lunch today."

"Oh," I said. "Yeah, of course." And while I was surprised by his request, given his latest encounter with the frying pan, I had to wonder how much this had to do with what Brennon had said yesterday about Steve cooking. I hadn't thought much about that, since Steve obviously hadn't wanted to talk about it, but my curiosity was piqued. "Do we need to stop by the store or anything?" I asked.

"I've already called in a grocery delivery," Steve replied, his ears turning a bit pink beneath the curls of his hair. "I was kind of banking on you being okay with it, and I didn't want to ruin the surprise."

I tried to find some sort of clue in Matthew's face, but he was suddenly stoic, though a light danced in his eyes. I doubted he would tell me anything if I asked, so I just thanked him and Indie for letting us stop by and took Steve by the arm, leading him back to the car as Captain followed close behind.

CHAPTER FOURTEEN

I didn't like the way he was breathing. Or rather, I didn't like the way he wasn't. Steve hadn't said much since arriving back at the apartment except to make sure all his ingredients were accounted for when the delivery arrived, and at first, I thought it was because he was focused on lunch. But the longer I sat on the couch, the dog at my side, the more I wondered if he was in more pain than he let on.

I'd never bruised any ribs, but I could imagine it wasn't a pleasant experience. Steve only took shallow breaths as he moved about the kitchen, sometimes pausing completely and leaning on his hands as he very slowly and deliberately filled his lungs.

He hadn't really gained any color back in his face, either, and that worried me too. It was only Thursday, barely halfway through the week I was looking after him. Was this the sort of thing I was supposed to be wary of? I got as far as looking up the number for the hospital, but I waited before I called. Maybe he was still just tired.

At the very least, I decided I probably shouldn't let him stand there and run the risk of injuring himself while cooking. "What is it you're making?" I asked.

Steve looked up, his arm wrapping around his ribcage almost unconsciously. "It's a surprise," he said.

How could I get him to let me do it without offending him? I was more than glad he was making the effort, but now was not the time. I needed to make him think it was his idea to let me take over. "Well I'm starving," I said. "I don't suppose you could hurry it up?"

He narrowed his eyes, but his glare was only so effective when he was very nearly smiling at the same time. "I didn't know you were such an impatient person," he said.

"Only when it comes to food."

"I'm getting there. It's been a while."

"That may be true," I said, "but that doesn't make me less hungry."

"Do you want to make it?" he asked, exasperation in his voice. *Perfect.*

"I do, actually," I said and joined him in the kitchen before he could argue. Taking him by the shoulders, I led him back to the couch then said, "Walk me through it, chef."

He seemed torn by the idea of not being the one to cook his fancy dish and by the desire to sit with Captain and rest, but he didn't argue with himself for long. "Cook the steak first," he said, settling on the couch. "There's a really good rub in the bag there. You'll be steaming the asparagus. Poaching the eggs."

This was surprisingly complicated for a man who pretended just yesterday he didn't cook. "I've never poached an egg before," I admitted. "Mom didn't do a lot of breakfast."

"I'll walk you through it," Steve replied. And then he smiled, and all of my worry flitted away. Somehow, that smile of his made me feel like I could do anything.

"Eggs Benedict. On a beef steak. Over asparagus. On top of sourdough bread." I sat on the couch, Captain licking my empty plate and my stomach and taste buds both delightfully satisfied. "Who would have thought?"

Steve smiled, and though he had only managed to eat half his portion so far, at least he wasn't appalled by my cooking ability with a dish I'd never attempted before. "It was always one of my favorites," he said softly.

"I'm sure it was better when you made it," I said.

He lifted one shoulder in a half-shrug, his eyes drooping a little. He was exhausted, and I was definitely glad I had taken over the job of doing the actual cooking. Besides, Steve had been an excellent coach, knowing the little nuances of the dish no recipe could have told me.

"Have you always been a cook?" I asked him.

His smile changed, a little strained now. "Every time I traveled somewhere new," he said, "I found someone to teach me something.

I always planned to retire early and open a restaurant, but…"

"But what?"

He fixed his dark eyes on me, his expression full of sadness. "I lost those dreams when I lost my sight," he said with a sigh.

Yeah, okay, I could see why that would make things harder. "That didn't stop you from making breakfast the other day," I argued.

"Pancakes and foie gras don't exactly compare," he said. "I can't fillet a fish if I can't see it. I can't even tell you how many times I've burned or cut myself just trying to make a sandwich."

"Any ten-year-old can tell you the same thing," I replied. "It just takes practice." But now it made sense why he would act as if he didn't know how to do any of this. He was probably so afraid of finding out that he really couldn't do it that he hadn't even tried.

He laughed a little, setting his plate on the end table next to him and turning to face me. "You're comparing me to a kid?" he said. "Very flattering."

"I'm just saying maybe you need to look at things differently, so to speak," I replied. "Take me, for example. My whole life I've had a plan and a goal, and suddenly I find myself with an endless supply of free time and possibilities. And I have no idea what to do about that." I frowned, not really sure how that was supposed to help anyone, least of all me. "But just because I have to change, it doesn't mean it's a bad thing. You just have to be open to adapting to whatever life throws at you."

As if on cue, my phone buzzed in my pocket. Hoping it was Brennon, I opened the text without checking who it was from. Gordon Hastings's message made my heart sink like a rock into my stomach: *I'm serious about being in your life, Lissa. I'm not going to give up.*

"What is it?" Steve asked, reaching out and finding my arm, though I was pretty sure he knew exactly who had texted me, given the sympathetic anger in his gaze.

"Can I ask you something?" I said, shoving my phone deep into the couch cushions. I needed a change of subject, and I needed it now. "What do you miss most?"

He sat up straighter, the little wrinkle appearing between his eyebrows. While he still held onto my wrist, his hold changed from comforting to a little too tight. "What?"

I knew it wasn't going to help anything, but my father put me in a bad mood. There wasn't any way it could get worse. "Since the accident," I said, "what do you miss most? Cooking? Skydiving? The freedom to go wherever whenever? Pretty girls?" That last one slipped out before I could stop myself.

Steve exhaled quickly through his nose and pressed his lips together, though I couldn't tell if he was angry or amused. Shaking his head, he pondered my question, probably trying to decide if he actually wanted to answer. "No one has asked me that before," he said. "I haven't really thought about it."

"But you must miss something more than the rest," I insisted and grabbed his hand. I didn't know why I was so desperate to know, but I was feeling lost. Ungrounded. I wanted to know what a man like Steve Evans considered important, because maybe I could grasp onto that and hold tight until I figured out what I was doing with my life.

Looking down, Steve took a slow, deep breath. "There are so many things," he said quietly. "Things I wish I could see again. Things I wish I could see for the first time. But what I really miss, what I would give anything to have back…" He lifted his eyes to mine, his gaze so focused that I could have sworn he saw me clearly. He'd gotten closer—maybe it was me who moved in my desperation to know—and I could see bits of green in his brown eyes I never would have noticed before.

"I miss the faces of the people I care about," he whispered finally, his eyes searching my face. How much did he see? "I miss seeing their happiness, their sadness, their worry, their contentment. I miss knowing what they feel." And he reached up, his fingers moving cautiously toward my face.

My phone buzzed again, practically vibrating the whole couch. Both of us jumped, and I scooted to the end of the couch as my heart started racing. If Gordon Hastings was trying to call me again, so help me… But the number on the screen was one I never thought I'd have to see again: *Cal Mikaelson*.

Curiosity hit the answer button before I could think things through. "Hello?" I breathed. Steve went back to picking at his food, and I stared at him as I tried to understand why my old boss would be calling me in the middle of the day.

"Lissa!" Cal's greeting came through loud and clear, making my jaw clench because his was the last voice I wanted to hear. "Sweetheart. How've you been?"

"What do you want, Cal?" I asked.

Steve glanced up at my annoyed tone, one eyebrow raised in interest as he tried to listen to my conversation. To make it easy for him, I turned on the speaker phone and held it out; I wanted someone else to witness the horror that was Cal Mikaelson.

"I've been thinking this last week," Cal said casually. I could almost picture him sitting in his fancy chair, tossing his baseball back and forth as he rested his feet on his desk. "I really don't like the way we left things."

"You promoted an imbecile instead of me," I replied.

"Yeah, Hamada's an idiot, it's true. But you gotta understand, babe—" I cringed as Steve scowled "—there were politics at work. Hamada's the CFO's nephew. I mean, if I didn't promote him, I'd lose my job."

He was part-owner of the company. I'd never heard such a load of bull in my life. "You mean if you put a woman in charge, people would question your manhood," I said. "I get it."

Steve snorted then immediately wrapped his arm around his ribs in pain.

Cal seemed to stumble over his words for a second, and then he muttered, "I'm calling because I made a mistake, Lissa."

"Oh?"

"I… You are…" He let out all his breath at once then said, "You're the only one who knows the Yun case, Lissa. Hamada's whole team has no idea what's going on, and Yun is threatening to take her money somewhere else."

Of course she was. Sonya Yun had come to me personally, and I'd spent months working on her file and putting together a proposal that could have tripled her capital. If any of the jerkwads at that company had bothered to listen to me, they would have known that. "I'm not sure what you expect me to do about that, Cal," I said, trying my best to sound absolutely clueless. It was how he saw me no matter what I did, so I might as well be what he expected.

"Come back, Lissa," he said. He actually sounded stressed. "I'll get my assistant to buy you a flight—where the hell even is she? Calif— why are you in California? Whatever. I'll pay to get you back to Boston tonight, and you can have Hamada's job. Please."

I stared at the phone in my hand, not entirely sure if I was hearing things right. Never in a million years would I have imagined Mikaelson begging, and yet he was offering to pay for an expensive last-minute flight to get me back and fix everything I'd left behind. I knew things would fall apart without me there, but I had no idea anyone would realize I was the reason everything had stayed together before.

"I don't know if that's the best idea," I muttered.

"I'll double your salary," he said. "Get you an assistant who actually knows what he's doing. Whatever you want. You have to come back, Montgomery."

I looked at Steve, but he had returned his focus to his food, though he was a lot more deliberate with his fork than he needed to be. Did he care about where I ended up? My stomach tied itself in a knot as I thought about that. If I left for Boston tonight and found someone else to stay with him, what would happen to him? Maybe he would go back to sulking around the apartment and barely eating his food. Maybe he would keep trying to cook and find a way to open that restaurant of his. Maybe he didn't even care, and my presence here was just because a doctor ordered it, and the moment I was gone he could get back to his own life instead of entertaining me and dealing with all my drama.

"Lissa," Cal said, "I'm desperate. At least think about it."

"I'll think about it," I muttered.

Mikaelson breathed a sigh of relief, and he sounded a whole lot happier as he said, "I knew I hired you for a reason. I'll check back in tomorrow, and I hope to hear good news."

The line clicked dead, and I sat there with my phone in my palm and my thoughts spinning fast enough to make me dizzy.

"Lissa, that's incredible news," Steve said.

I jumped, not because I'd forgotten he was there, but because he sounded so cold. Empty. "He just wants me to fix his problems for him," I said softly, looking at my phone instead of him.

"He realizes he made a mistake letting you go," he corrected. "He recognizes your value, and that's an important thing to have. You should go."

I turned to him. "What?"

He almost looked angry as he sat there, his gaze anywhere but on me. "That's an amazing opportunity, and you shouldn't give that up."

"But you need—"

"Don't factor me into this," he practically growled. "I've already spent too much time keeping you from your own life. Don't make me feel guilty for keeping you away from this."

So he didn't care. That was…illuminating. And I had no idea why that hurt so much.

Rolling his eyes, Steve set his plate on the side table and shook his head. "At least give it some thought," he muttered. "I'm…I'm exhausted after yesterday, so I'm going to take a nap." He whistled softly, and the dog immediately jumped up onto the couch with him.

Guess that was my cue. The moment I stood, Steve stretched out on the couch and closed his eyes as Captain settled at his side. Thoroughly banished and feeling awful, I gripped my phone and wandered to Brennon's bedroom. Steve didn't care what I did. More than the thought of working for Mikaelson again, that fact made me sick to my stomach. I thought we were friends. I thought I had gotten through to him and connected with him. I thought I was starting to figure out who this guy was, but apparently I was wrong.

I called Brennon before I could stop myself, curling up in a ball under the covers of his bed and hoping he wasn't too busy to answer. I needed someone who knew my life predicament, and at the moment, Brennon was the only other one who even knew I had quit in the first place. Besides, we were dating. Sort of. Maybe we weren't in love— *ha*—but I was pretty sure Brennon cared enough about me to care about something like this.

But the call went to his voicemail. He was probably in a meeting. He would probably call me back as soon as he was out. But instead of leaving a message, I hung up and immediately dialed my mom.

Her answering machine made me groan: "This is Moira! Paul and I are on a cruise for our anniversary, so we won't get back to you until after Christmas. Aloha!"

"Mom," I said to the machine, "don't tell the world your house is empty. That's a good way to get robbed."

She didn't tell me she was going on a cruise. She didn't tell me she wasn't going to be around for Christmas! What, was I going to find out when I showed up for the holidays and found the house deserted? But even as I lay there in a stranger's bed in an apartment that wasn't mine, I knew what my mom would argue: *You never come home for Christmas, Lissa. You're always working.* I couldn't remember the last time I saw my mother for more than a weekend, and in the last month, I had talked more to my nightmare of a father than to the woman who raised me on her own.

What a terrible daughter I had turned out to be.

My phone battery was practically dead, but I had one last call to make, though I already knew he wouldn't answer. I just wanted to hear his voice, because he somehow managed to make me feel like nothing could go wrong.

"You've reached Seth," his message said. "If you even think about bothering me while I'm on my honeymoon, you'll have me to answer to. Leave a message at your own risk."

"Hey, Seth," I said quietly, holding my phone as tight as my voice sounded. "I know I shouldn't be calling you, but I..." I what? I needed my big brother. "I need your advice, and you always know what to say. I, uh, I quit my job. Last week. Mikaelson promoted someone else instead of me, and I snapped. I've been staying in San Francisco because there's nothing to go back to in Boston, and I've been looking around trying to figure out what I want to do with my life. But Mikaelson just called me. He's realized how much he needs me, and he's practically begging me to go back. Offered me double my old salary and control of my own team. It's everything I ever wanted and worked for. So why is it so hard for me to say yes? I don't..." I swallowed, curling up into an even tighter ball. "I don't know what to do, Seth. You've always had everything figured out. Since the day I met you, you knew exactly what you were doing with your life and who you wanted to be. I wish I knew how to do that. I wish I had a plan. Or even just a direction."

I felt awful. Like the realization of what I'd done in quitting my job was just barely hitting me in full force and I was just realizing how lost I really was. My entire life I had had a plan. I knew exactly where I wanted to be and what I wanted to do, and suddenly all of that felt so wrong. I didn't want to work for Cal Mikaelson no matter how much money he offered me. Nothing would change, and everyone in that office would pretend I had no idea what I was doing and that I was just there to look pretty and make the office seem more inclusive.

I didn't even know if I wanted to stay in California. Brennon wasn't exactly begging me to stay, and while the Davenports would be thrilled to add me to their collection, I would be the odd man out, the one they took pity on and included when they should be spending time with each other. Seth would tell me to stay, but he just got married. He had a new family to worry about, and I didn't want to take him away from Catherine, who was everything he deserved in a wife.

Even if I went back to Vermont, Mom had someone new. She couldn't even be bothered to tell her only daughter she was spending a month on the ocean over the most family-centered holiday.

And Steve? He didn't want me around any more than he had in the beginning.

I was alone. I would always be alone.

"Tell me what to do, Seth," I whispered and hung up the phone.

And for the first time in years, since crying was a weakness I couldn't show in my line of work, I pressed my face into the pillow and sobbed.

CHAPTER FIFTEEN

My head ached. Years of bottled up tears could do that to a girl. I didn't know how long I had been out, but I woke to a room darker than it had been before I cried myself to sleep. Though maybe that was because of the rain pattering on the window… I dug my phone out from under the covers to check the time, but it had finally died. Brennon had an old-fashioned alarm clock across the room, but my eyes were so blurry I could barely see it let alone the hands on its face. Oh man, my head really hurt, and that barking was not helping.

Barking.

Lifting my head, I glared at the dog who stood in the doorway. "Be quiet," I mumbled.

He just barked again.

"Go bother Steve." He could probably handle a trip down the elevator on his own. He certainly didn't think he needed me around to help him.

Captain refused to stop, even taking a couple of steps into the room. But he wouldn't come any closer, and he kept glancing back to the main room.

The blood drained from my face, my heart stuttering in my chest. What if…?

"What's wrong?" I asked the dog, struggling to my feet.

His barking got more urgent as he backed away, making sure I followed.

I hurried my steps. "Steve?"

Captain jumped onto the couch and licked Steve's face.

Steve didn't move.

"Oh my God," I gasped. "Steve!" He was ashen, his lips almost blue, and I touched my fingers to his neck, fearing the worst. His heart still beat, but it was way too fast and weak. "Steve, wake up!"

911. But my phone was dead. I didn't have time to charge it. Brennon didn't have a landline. Neither did Catherine.

"Steve, please wake up."

Steve had a phone. Somewhere. More tears filling my eyes, I stumbled into Steve's room and searched in the darkness. Where would a blind man leave his most prized possession? *In the drawer.* I tore open his nightstand, letting out a shaky breath when I saw his almost fully charged phone lying on top.

I could barely dial the numbers, but when the phone started ringing, I hurried back to Steve and kept trying to wake him up.

"911 emergency response."

"I need an ambulance," I gasped and stammered out Brennon's address. "He's not responding. I don't—he was hit by a car last week and I think something's wrong. Please hurry."

And then I collapsed against the couch, and though the woman on the phone kept talking to me, I didn't know what she said to me. I just grabbed Steve's cold hand behind me and prayed I didn't lose him.

If Catherine's cousin Lanna hadn't driven me to the hospital, I didn't think I would have made it there on my own. It was a miracle I got a hold of her at all, and I'd never been more grateful for the internet and the fact that her husband was moderately famous in the art dealing world.

"Do you want me to stay?" Lanna asked softly as we sat in the hospital parking lot. She hadn't asked many questions aside from the necessary ones, for which I was grateful. I wasn't sure if I had the energy to tell her more than my friend was in the hospital and I needed a ride, but she seemed to understand more than I would have expected.

I took a slow breath, but it didn't loosen the tightness in my chest. "I'll be okay," I lied. "You should get back home."

"Hang on." She reached for something from her purse, and I stared at the brightly lit hospital through the rain, trying to work up the courage to go inside. None of the paramedics would tell me if he was going to be okay. They wouldn't let me ride in the ambulance. It had been almost an hour, and I had no idea what I was going to find inside.

"Here," Lanna said and handed me a little sheet of paper with a bunch of phone numbers. Every single one of the Davenports, including Lanna's parents. "We're all just a phone call away."

I nearly broke down into tears there in the car, but I bit my cheek and held it back. Not until I knew whether he was going to be okay. I wouldn't cry unless I had a real reason. "Thank you," I whispered. Lanna pulled me in for an awkward side hug, and then I hurried out into the rain and through the front doors.

Shoulders damp and hair dripping, I shook as I slowly approached the front desk. There were only a couple of things the woman could tell me. Either Steve was recovering, or he was dead. "Hi," I breathed, forcing myself to ask. The waiting and wondering would only make things worse. "I'm here for Steven Evans. He's... He was brought in about an hour ago."

Taking a moment to look me over, she nodded and typed a few things into her computer. And then her carefully calm expression faltered, and she took an extra-long time to look back up at me. "I'm going to send you to the emergency room," she said softly. "I'll let them know you're coming."

Bad news. They only had bad news for me. But I nodded and turned in the direction she pointed. My feet felt so heavy, and I couldn't help but remember the last time I'd been here. Brennon at my side. I'd only been here to reassure him that everything would be okay, and there was nothing to worry about. Now there was everything to worry about, and I was alone. Completely alone.

Oh. I probably should have called Brennon.

Pausing just outside the ER, I searched through Steve's contacts—hovering my thumb over Amelia's name—and found Brennon's number listed as "Bigshot." Though the call went to his voicemail again, this time I did leave a message.

"Something's happened," I said, trying to get enough sound in my voice so he could actually hear me. "Steve is in the hospital. I need..." Why was it so hard to say? I needed him. I couldn't go through this alone. "You need to be here, Brennon."

The same doctor as the last time greeted me inside, his expression hard. "You're here for Mr. Evans?" he asked. What had Brennon called him? Dave.

I sank against the wall, too anxious to hold myself up. "Please tell me he's okay," I whispered. If he wasn't, I would never forgive myself. I was supposed to watch him. My only purpose even being there was to make sure something like this didn't happen.

Doctor Dave cleared his throat and gestured toward a waiting room, where only a couple of other people sat, and he directed me to take a chair there. Definitely bad news. Sitting next to me, he cleared his throat again then said, "Steve went into hypovolemic shock."

What did that mean? I shook my head.

"He was bleeding internally," he explained. "And he lost more than a liter. We had to operate to repair the torn vessels in his abdomen."

"Tell me he's okay," I said again.

But the doctor's expression didn't change, and he took a deep breath. "It's too early to tell," he said. "We're doing some tests to see how much damage there may have been to his organs, but we will keep you updated."

"But he was fine," I said. "Maybe a little tired, but he said he was fine. I didn't think... He was fine."

Shrugging, he rose to his feet and put his hand on my shoulder. "Most likely there was some injury we missed when he was here last," he said gently. "Something could have aggravated it, or he may have ignored the symptoms. It wouldn't be the first time."

I tensed, staring up at him. "What do you mean?"

He pursed his lips, glancing around the almost empty room. "I need to get back to Mr. Evans," he said, his voice low. "We will keep you updated."

He left me alone on my plastic chair, horrid thoughts running through my head as I wondered just how many times Steve had ended up in this emergency room.

Brennon showed up at nine. I could hear him outside the waiting room, demanding information, but I was too exhausted to go find him and tell him what little I knew. Eventually he was forced into the waiting room, and he ran his hands through his hair and almost burst back through the door before he turned around and saw me where I sat on the floor with my back against the wall.

"Lissa," he gasped and rushed over. "Lissa, tell me what's going on."

"He's out of surgery," I mumbled as I hugged my knees. I'd been sitting in this room for hours, and that little bit of information hadn't been enough to calm me down. I could barely breathe, my whole chest tight and twisted, and I knew I shouldn't have been angry at Brennon, but I was. I was angry it took him so long to care about his friend and angry that he hadn't been here with me to help me breathe. No job was worth ignoring something like this. My body ached from being so tense, and I still had no idea if Steve was even going to survive.

"He's going to be okay, right?"

This was why I was never going to find love. My entire life, I had always come second. "I don't know, Brennon," I said weakly.

Moaning, he threw his jacket against one of the chairs and started pacing. "How did this happen?" he asked the room. Then me. "Lissa, how could you—"

"He was fine," I snapped. "He said so himself." And I didn't need Brennon to blame me too. I was doing just fine with that on my own.

"He also said he was eating, but then I found him half-dead on the floor," Brennon growled back. "I trusted you to look after him so something like this wouldn't happen again."

I jumped up, and though I wasn't in my intimidation heels, Brennon still stumbled back a step. "Don't you dare," I said, keeping my voice low. "I have spent the last few days doing everything I possibly could to keep that man not just alive but *living*, so don't you dare blame me for this."

Someone coughed in the doorway, and both of us turned to see a nurse awkwardly trying to get our attention. "Mr. Ashworth," she said, her voice a little wary, "you can see him now."

Brennon immediately grabbed my hand, his anger apparently gone. Though I still didn't like how easily he jumped to the conclusion that somehow I had caused this—even if he was right—I held on tightly. I needed the human contact, and knowing I wasn't alone anymore took a little of the weight off my chest.

Together we followed the nurse into a small room in the ICU, and though Brennon went straight in, I hung back at the door. Steve looked so small compared to the monitors and the IV tubes and the ventilator keeping him alive. Despite the bag of crimson flowing into his hand, he still looked too pale. Not alive enough.

"Hey buddy," Brennon said softly and pulled the one chair closer to the bed so he could sit next to him. "You can't scare us like this. Not again."

Steve was still unconscious, and fear spiked in my chest again. What if he didn't wake up? What if I was too late? What if—

"He's lucky," Doctor Dave said behind me, making me jump. "If you hadn't made the call when you did, there's no way he would have pulled through this time."

I stared at him and took a second to make sure I heard him right. "He's going to be okay?" I asked, though I wasn't sure any sound actually came out.

Doctor Dave smiled. "Thanks to you."

I met Brennon's gaze, and tears filled his eyes as he watched me.

"Lissa," he said, pulling his eyebrows together. "I'm..." I couldn't blame him for being angry with me. Not when I was angry with myself for the same thing. But I wasn't sure I had the energy to deal with his apology right now.

"I should go check on the dog," I muttered and headed down the hall.

"Lissa!" Shiny shoes squeaking on the tile, Brennon caught up to me easily and took my arm as he slid to a stop in front of me. "Lissa, please. I'm sorry. I didn't mean..."

I took a steadying breath that didn't really do me much good. "Don't worry about it."

"Let me go check on the dog," he continued. I wasn't expecting that, and I stared at him as he added, "You'd probably rather be here with Steve anyway." What was that supposed to mean? He bit his tongue and looked down at the ground as if fighting against something else that tried to come out of his mouth. "Let me know when he wakes up, okay?" he said finally.

I nodded, and then he was gone. Almost mechanically, I returned to Steve's room and took Brennon's place in the chair. He was going to be okay. I exhaled, my breath shaking from me but taking some of my stress with it. "You're going to be okay," I repeated out loud, even if Steve couldn't hear me.

And when I took his hand, this time his fingers were warm.

I didn't often complain about my height. Five-foot-ten wasn't completely unheard of, but it definitely set me apart from the average woman. It made buying clothes harder than it should have been, and I always had to opt for the more expensive extra legroom seats on airplanes. But the worst part about being tall was trying to sleep in a little hospital armchair. I simply didn't fit, and around three in the morning, I decided to give up trying and go find some coffee to keep me awake.

Before I even moved, I froze and looked toward the bed, instinct telling me something was different. The room was dim, but Steve's eyes were open and focused right on me. He was awake. And though that made me happier than I thought I could be, I still didn't move. I didn't know what to say to him, not when all I could think about was the fact that even Brennon wasn't surprised Steve was here. He had obviously been in this situation more than a couple of times.

So I just sat in my chair and met Steve's gaze, wondering what he might be thinking as he watched me.

After a few minutes, a nurse came into the room to check on him. "You're awake," she said happily and jotted down a couple of numbers from the monitor. "Let's get you off that ventilator, okay?" She undid the tape keeping it in place then asked, "Ready?" Steve must have given her some sort of sign, because she started to pull, and though Steve choked and coughed, making me cringe, the nurse seemed satisfied once she pulled the tube free. "Good job," she told him, scribbling a couple more numbers then disappearing, leaving the room quiet again.

"You look like crap," Steve said as soon as she was gone, a bit hoarse but definitely alive.

I shrugged. "Yeah, well—wait, you can't even see me," I said. Especially with the room this dark.

Rolling his eyes, he adjusted himself a little without looking away from me. "I don't need to see you to know," he said. "You should have gone home, Lissa."

He didn't want me here. That stung more than I thought it would, since it wasn't exactly a new revelation.

"You need to sleep," he clarified quickly, as if he knew my thoughts. "Somewhere other than a hospital chair."

A little burst of warmth blossomed inside me, and I pulled the chair back to the side of the bed to get closer to him. Was I wrong? "Sleep is for wimps," I said. "Besides, I wasn't about to leave you here by yourself."

Glancing around, Steve swallowed then asked, "Where's Bren?"

"He's at home taking care of Captain."

"I'm sorry, Lissa."

As much as I wanted to hear that, apprehension filled my gut, and I couldn't bring myself to look at him. Was he sorry that I spent all night in a chair, or was he sorry that he let himself end up nearly dying? "Did you know?" I whispered. "Did you know you were sick?"

I looked up when he touched the back of his finger to my cheek. A tear hung in his eye, clinging to his eyelashes as he gazed at me. "No," he said. "I told you I would never lie to you. I meant it."

I took his hand and pressed it against my cheek, still needing the comfort of human contact. "What did the doctor mean when he said you might have been ignoring the symptoms?" I asked. "Has something like this happened before?"

He closed his eyes, though he kept his hand firmly against my skin. "Just after I moved in with Brennon," he said, "the elevators were out for a couple of days. I needed some fresh air—to get away—but I slipped on the stairs. Fell nearly the whole way down." He took a slow, difficult breath. "I already hated that Brennon felt the need to give up half his condo for me, and I didn't want to bother him with a few bumps and bruises. I honestly had no idea I was bleeding because I couldn't see it."

"But there had to have been other signs."

Shrugging, he opened his eyes and fixed them on me. "I thought the dizziness was from the blindness," he said. "That I was just tired after my brush with starvation. I swear to God I didn't know anything was wrong until I passed out in the middle of the kitchen, no matter what Brennon and Dr. Thurston think."

Relief washed over me. "So you didn't...?" I couldn't bring myself to finish that question. How low had Steve gotten?

He shook his head, dropping his hand but keeping a firm hold on mine. "As soon as I realized there was still someone who wanted me in this world," he whispered, "I couldn't. Bren is literally the only reason I'm still alive. Well, Bren and you, Lissa."

My heart skittered a bit, but then his eyelids drooped. "You should get some sleep," I said, gently setting his hand back on the bed.

"You should too," he replied as half his mouth twisted into a smile. "But you probably won't do that, will you?"

"Nope."

"Then at least go get some food," he said, making the warmth in my chest grow. How could I have ever thought he wanted me to leave when he looked at me like that? "I'll be here when you get back."

I hadn't eaten anything since Steve's Steak Benedict, and though I knew I needed to get something in me, my stomach was still slowly untangling itself from the knots it had twisted into during those hours I wondered if Steve was still alive. Day-old mac and cheese from the hospital cafeteria just didn't seem all that appetizing after the week I'd had.

He was going to be okay. I had to keep telling myself that over and over as I pushed my food around my plate, my head resting in my hand and my body aching and sore. Despite everything he had been through, I was quickly learning Steve was a fighter. This little setback would likely just make him stronger, and I wouldn't have to spend the rest of my life wondering if he was still alive and kicking. He was going to be okay.

I had to wonder what would happen to him now. Maybe he needed another week of supervision. Maybe they would just keep him at the hospital until they were sure he'd sustained no other damage. I hoped not. Being subjected to this food was bad enough, but Steve didn't need to be cooped up. He needed to be outside in the fresh air, re-learning how to live in a different light. Maybe he couldn't see like he used to, but that shouldn't stop him from living the life he loved.

If they sent him home, if he needed someone to look after him, would they trust me to do it again? I'd nearly gotten him killed because I didn't look closely enough at the signs. But the bigger question was would Steve even want me to? We'd become friends over the last several days, but I think I annoyed him more than I should. I forced him to eat, and I pushed him to be better and break through barriers he'd put up himself. If I were him, I'd rather count on myself to make me change, not some lunatic who had somehow managed to fall for my roommate after a single brunch date.

A brown paper bag suddenly appeared on the table in front of me, and I stared at it in alarm before I realized someone had set it there and it hadn't just popped up out of thin air. "I thought you might want some real food," Brennon said softly, taking the chair opposite me.

I sat up, blinking away the dryness in my eyes before I peeked inside the bag. "What is it?" I asked as I reached in and pulled out the best-looking hamburger I had ever seen.

"You haven't had a burger until you've had the Maverick," Brennon said with a little smile.

I had to take a bite before the sight of it put me into a food coma, and it was still sizzling hot, though the coleslaw above the patty helped cool it down and made it altogether delicious. "Bren," I said, my mouth still full, "it's like four in the morning."

"I like when you call me Bren." He sat with one arm over the back of his chair, the other resting on the table with his fingers nearly close enough for me to touch them. "The manager over there owed me a favor," he explained as I kept eating.

I couldn't decide if it was the burger lightening my mood or the fact that he'd called in a favor—it had to have been quite the favor—just to get me some good food in the middle of the night. Either way, I took back any bad thought I'd had about the guy over the last twelve hours. "Thank you, Bren," I said quietly. I would have reached for his hand, but my own was smothered in sauce.

He pulled his hands into his lap instead and watched me eat for a second, and then he took a deep breath and asked the question he had probably been wanting to ask all night: "How's Steve?"

Setting the last few bites of burger back on the paper cover it had come in, I took a moment to wipe my hands clean before I answered. I was still a little afraid that if I said it out loud, it would somehow turn out not to be true. "He was awake for a few minutes," I said, and Brennon's shoulders relaxed. "He's asleep again, but everyone is optimistic." I reached for the burger, too hungry to stay away for long.

"Thank God," he breathed, letting even more tension out with his exhale. "I'm sure he was happy to see you when he woke up."

My hands froze halfway to my mouth. He was doing it again, saying things that didn't make sense. "What is that supposed to mean?" I asked, maybe a little rougher than I should have been.

Laughing softly, Brennon shook his head and met my gaze, looking at me as if he couldn't understand how I could possibly have no clue what he was trying to say. "You don't see it," he said, more to himself than to me. Louder, he continued, "I have known that man for years, Lissa. He may have been popular, but even before the accident he barely tolerated people and couldn't give a crap what other people thought. And I don't think I've ever seen him try as hard to impress someone as he has this last week."

The burger slipped from my fingers and onto the table in a scattered mess, but I didn't care. I couldn't move, could barely think as I kept my full focus on Brennon. The guy had barely been around Steve this week, so what could he possibly be talking about?

"Don't take this the wrong way," he said, "but if he had met you before the accident, when he could actually see you, he wouldn't have given you the time of day."

Well that was…painful. "I'm having a hard time not seeing an insult in that," I grumbled, hoping he was getting to some sort of point. I was too tired for a conversation like this.

Brennon grinned, shaking his head again as he glanced around the mostly deserted cafeteria. "You're beautiful, Lissa," he said, turning his grey-blue eyes back to me. Suddenly I felt like I was floating. "Extremely. And if he had been able to see you, he would have assumed you would use that to your full advantage, and he would have dismissed you before he could figure out you're not remotely like the women who do."

My voice was lodged in my throat, stuck there by the combination of pleasure and horror his words gave me. I'd never cared much about my appearance, mostly because it usually got me into trouble, and I hated vanity more than most things. But hearing Brennon say stuff like that was enough to make a girl swoon, and I very badly wanted to jump across the table and kiss him in gratitude. The only thing keeping me in my chair was my desperation to hear the rest of what he had to say, because somehow, I knew he wasn't finished.

"Thanks?" I said, unsure exactly how to respond.

Brennon's smile warmed even more. "You care about the important things," he said. "The things you can actually control."

But what did this have to do with Steve?

"The dog's fine, by the way."

I nodded, grateful for the update but still focused on the last topic. It felt important.

"Steve picked out the collar, didn't he?" Brennon continued.

Again, I nodded and wondered if I was missing something or just too exhausted to see the point of this little bit of conversation.

Smiling a little, Brennon shook his head and looked right into my eyes. "I have no idea how he managed it, but he really did pick the exact shade. We should go see if he's awake," he added, scooting back with a harsh scraping of metal on linoleum as he rose. He held out his hand, and though I slipped my fingers between his, something felt wrong. Different.

I followed Brennon, my thoughts too slow and jumbled to piece together. I needed sleep, but I had no intention of leaving the hospital until I was absolutely sure Steve would be okay. I could sleep later, even if that meant I couldn't fully comprehend what was happening around me now. It was a good thing Brennon knew the way to go, because if I had gotten in that elevator on my own, I would have stared at the rows of buttons with no clue which to push until I rested enough to clear my head. But he pressed the number three, and soft music played overhead, lulling me into a comfortable haze.

"Hey buddy," Brennon said, and I realized with a jolt we had already reached Steve's little room. Had I just fallen asleep while walking? "Good to see you awake!"

"Sorry for the scare," Steve replied.

I shook my head a little, blinking hard to try to keep my eyes open. I wanted to see him. I wanted to make sure he had more color in his face and that he was actually getting better.

"Think you can get her to go home and get some sleep?" one of them asked the other. I wasn't sure which.

"I can try," said the other, "but she's stubborn. Probably more stubborn than you."

"I have an idea."

"Come lie down here, Lissa."

A hand pulled me forward.

Someone helped me settle on something soft, something warm, and everything else disappeared as the longest day of my life slowly came to an end.

CHAPTER SIXTEEN

I woke to the sound of voices, one much louder than the other, like a rumble right in my ear. I still felt like I could have slept for hours, but the sunlight streaming into the room was enough to bring me back to reality. I had too many people to worry about to spend all my time sleeping.

"Good morning," the louder voice said. I could feel him in my ear along with a strong, rhythmic thump.

"We were wondering if you were ever going to wake up," the other voice said lightly.

Wait. That farther voice sounded like Brennon. I opened my eyes, and for a moment all I could see was pale blue beneath my palm. A hospital gown. And though I was still trying to wake up, I realized exactly where I was. Lifting my head, I found myself just a few inches from Steve's face. "Oh."

His characteristic wrinkle appeared between his eyebrows as he gazed at me and repeated, "Oh," as if he wasn't sure what to do with my soft word.

I wasn't sure what to do with it either. "How did I get here?" He was thin, yes, but there was still a decent bit of muscle on his chest beneath my palm, making him a very comfortable pillow. Surprising.

Steve smiled, the dimples in his scruffy cheeks tightening my chest a little bit. "We were debating how much you'd remember," he said. "You owe me ten bucks, dude."

"Fine."

I turned my head and found Brennon lounging in the chair, his legs over one arm and looking much too handsome for a guy who had probably slept as poorly as I had. He was so good at his emotional masks that it was almost impossible to tell when he was wearing one. "What time is it?" I asked him.

"Time for me to get to work," he replied. "Walk me to the door?"

I eagerly agreed, though climbing out of the hospital bed was harder than it apparently was to get into it, and I managed to bump Steve's incision on his stomach and get a hiss of pain out of him. "Sorry," I gasped and scrambled away as quickly as I could to avoid hurting him more.

He was too busy grimacing to reply.

Taking my hand, Brennon paused in the doorway and looked back toward the bed. "I know I said it before," he said, "but I'm still mad at you for not telling Lissa you were in pain. But I'm glad you're okay."

Steve just waved a couple of fingers.

I worried I had done some serious damage, but Brennon gently pulled me out into the hall before I could go into hysterics. *Hysterics?* I needed a good slap to the face and some strong coffee. And I probably didn't need to be sleeping with my head on the arm of a man who had very nearly died less than twenty-four hours earlier.

"They'll probably keep him under observation for a few more hours," Brennon told me as we slowly walked down the quiet hall. "But Dave—Dr. Thurston—said there's a chance he'll be discharged later today."

"Really? So soon?"

His smile was off, almost sad as he looked at me. "That's assuming he'll have you to look after him while I'm at work."

I wasn't sure that was a good idea. "Brennon," I said, "he almost died while I was looking after him. I don't think—"

"That wasn't your fault."

"It wasn't Steve's fault either."

Brennon raised his eyebrows, a little caught off guard by my response, but his smile shifted into something a little more real. "Nevertheless," he said, "Dr. Thurston is confident in your abilities, so if you're willing..."

"Of course I'm willing," I replied.

Pausing even though we were nowhere near the hospital entrance, Brennon pulled me aside to clear the hallway and spent a long several seconds just looking at me, reading something in my face. "He'll be in good hands then," he said finally and pressed a long kiss to my fore-head.

It took me a good five seconds of him walking down the hall for me to process what had just happened. "Wait!" I shouted and hurried after him. Luckily, he paused, because I was still too sleepy to run very far. "Brennon, why did that feel like a goodbye kiss?"

Was he… Wait, were those tears pooling in his eyes? Brennon laughed softly, stuffing his hands into his pockets as he stood there next to a cart with a portable ventilator like the one they'd used on Steve. "I told you when we first met," he said, his voice cracking a little as he stared at the ground. "I don't believe in love."

That was bull if ever I'd heard any. Brennon Ashworth had abso-lutely been in love before, and I had a feeling it had something to do with the girl in the photo by his bed. Whoever she was, she had hurt him. Badly. "Brennon," I said.

"Even if I did," he continued, and a tear slipped from his eye as he blinked and looked up at me. "Even if I did, there's no point falling for a woman when she's already in love with someone else."

I stared at him as my brain tried to keep up. "In love?" I asked. "With *Steve?* You're kidding, right?" I didn't fall in love. People didn't fall in love with me. It was just how things went for me.

Brennon shrugged. "Just because I don't believe in love doesn't mean I can't recognize it when I see it."

"But—"

"I like you, Lissa. A lot." He said this as he slowly backed away toward the exit. "I think we could be really good friends. And I think you deserve more in a job than someone who just wants you to fix his problems for him." How did he even know about that?

"Brennon," I choked, but I couldn't seem to get my feet to follow him.

"There's no one in the world who deserves happiness more than Steve Evans," he said, and he was getting too far away. "And being around you has made him happier than I've seen him in years." The elevator opened behind him, and he stepped inside without looking away from me. "Don't hurt him," he said, and then he was gone.

I stood there in an empty hospital hallway more confused than I'd ever been in my life, and I had no idea what to do to fix it.

So I did the only thing I could do and slowly made my way back to Steve's room, desperately trying to get myself into one piece before I fell apart and just ran and hid until I could figure out exactly what was going on inside me. Brennon thought I was in love with Steve? But I barely knew the guy, and I'd spent the last week totally into Brennon, not his roommate. And Steve couldn't possibly be in love with me, or he wouldn't have said I should go back to Boston. Unless… Unless that was more of a selfless act than it seemed? Maybe he thought me going back to Boston was best for me, that it would make me happy. Could Brennon's words possibly be true?

When I reached the room, Steve was sitting up, holding a little plastic cup of red Jell-O and examining it so intently that it was like he was trying to figure out its exact chemical makeup.

"You know you're supposed to eat your food, not play with it, right?" I asked quietly.

Wow, his smile was beautiful, especially now that he had color back in his face. "I'm just trying to decide if it's worth a little bargaining," he said.

"Yeah?"

He nodded, pursing his lips as if deep in thought. "Yeah. I think it might work. I'll eat this."

I settled in the little chair, surprised by how comfortable it was. Had it always been so soft? "Good."

Holding up a finger, he tried very hard to focus his gaze on me but came a little short, missing me by a couple of inches because I probably blended in with the chair. "I'll eat it," he repeated, "but only if you promise to make me something spectacular when we get home."

When we get home. That phrase had a nice ring to it. "I'm not sure I have the ability to concoct spectacular," I said as a warmth spread through me, starting from my chest and expanding outward until even my toes tingled with it.

Steve cocked his head, the wrinkle deep between his eyebrows and his lips in a smile he just couldn't seem to get rid of. "Everything you make is spectacular, Lissa," he said softly.

Maybe Brennon wasn't completely crazy.

Steve tripped twice on the short walk from the cab to the apartment. He blamed it on the meds; I blamed it on the fact that he knew I would be there to catch him.

"You're going to injure yourself again," I said, steadying him.

He easily maneuvered my hand so his arm could slip around mine. "I think you'll have to guide me," he said playfully, his face distractingly close to mine.

Either Brennon had had an eye-opening talk with his roommate too, or I had seriously missed some signals from the guy. Either way, everything felt different as we walked to the elevator. This was no longer a man who felt guilty about me being stuck there with him, and I couldn't argue against Brennon's logic. Not when Steve gave me that smoldering—albeit unfocused—look as the elevator doors opened onto our floor.

"You don't have to stay, you know," he said softly as I dug through my purse for the keys.

I grinned. "I don't? Oh good."

I turned to walk away, but Steve reached out, running his hand along my arm until he could grab my hand. "But I hope you do," he added.

I didn't know what my plans were, but I did know I had no intention of going far. Not anymore. Unlocking the door with my free hand and pushing it open, I was just about to tell him so when something furry darted between my legs and jumped up onto Steve.

"Captain!" I shouted and reached out, barely managing to catch Steve before he was knocked to the ground. "Bad dog!"

But Steve lowered himself to his knees and let the dog frantically lick his face as he rubbed his neck. "Don't listen to the mean lady," he said in a ridiculous baby voice that left me standing there with wide eyes. Never in a million years would I have expected that tone from the likes of Steve Evans. "You're a very, very good dog, aren't you?"

"He lives up to his name," I said with a small smile. If not for that pup waking me up, I might not have found Steve in time to save him. "You could call him a hero."

Though he still stroked the dog's golden fur, Steve looked up at me with his mouth in a thin line and that wrinkle between his eyebrows that seemed to be there every time he looked at me now. "I disagree," he said.

"That dog saved your life," I argued.

"*You* saved my life, Lissa."

My heart pounding in my ears and my face burning, I hurried deeper into the apartment, Steve right behind me. The dog had been a nice distraction, but eventually we were going to have to talk about what was going to happen with the two of us. I would have to figure out exactly why my chest felt so tight and why I couldn't seem to get myself to look away from the man for more than a few seconds. I had to figure out if Brennon was right.

But first I had to breathe. Find some way to build a little courage.

"You need to take your meds," I said, pulling the bottle from my purse and filling a glass with water.

Steve swallowed the pills without complaint, but he kept his eyes on me. I could sense words on the tip of his tongue, and I wasn't sure which topic he would choose. I wasn't sure which would be easiest, though the longer I looked into his face, the more I realized the future wasn't all that hard to figure out. There was something special about Steve. Something about the way he made me feel like I was important and valuable and worth listening to. The more I thought about it, the more I wondered if there was anyone in the world who had ever made me feel like I mattered as much as this man did.

How could I have doubted my feelings for him?

"You will stay, won't you?" The poor guy actually looked a little afraid as he asked that question, though he tried to cover it up by filling up his glass again.

I couldn't help but grin, which made all of it easier to stomach. I definitely didn't like being so serious all the time, and I decided to lighten the mood. Steve's life was dark enough already. "I dunno," I said as casually as I could manage. "I have a pretty good offer at my old job. I could go back to having my boss spend every meeting staring at my chest and make six figures just standing there looking pretty."

I couldn't have planned it better. Steve choked halfway through taking a sip of water, and his spit take spewed all over Captain, who cowered a little in alarm. He coughed a couple of times, pressing a hand to his stitches, and then he gasped, "Six fi—Lissa, why aren't you on a plane right now?"

I burst out laughing, grabbing a kitchen towel and tossing it over Steve's head, and then I said the only definite thing I knew when it came to my career: "I don't care about the money." Besides, I was pretty sure there was no way Mikaelson could *actually* offer me double my previous salary, no matter what he promised. "Nothing's changed. I want what I do to mean something, and I want to actually enjoy it."

He wasn't convinced, and as he stood there holding the towel, he looked ready to jump into a long argument about why I was making a mistake by not plugging my phone in to charge so I could call Cal and tell him I was coming to save his sorry butt from total ruin.

"I'd much rather be here," I told him and placed my hand on his stubbly cheek.

He immediately put his hand over mine, myriad emotions flitting rapidly across his face as his eyes searched the dimness of his sight for something. He reached up, carefully brushing his fingers across my nose and cheeks, taking in as many of my features as he could. "I wish I could see you," he whispered, looking completely miserable. "Even just a little bit."

I had no idea if that was even possible, but that wasn't about to stop me from trying. Taking both his hands, I led him close to the window where sunlight streamed in, almost blinding as I put his back to the glass so the light was completely on my face. Then I held my breath, because as much as I hated how often people called me pretty, I desperately hoped *he* thought so.

Steve was silent for a long time, his eyes roving every inch of my face in search of details. He kept leaning closer, I kept losing my ability to think rationally, and when he opened his mouth, his soft words nearly undid me. "Why didn't you tell me you were beautiful, Lissa?" he asked.

"I never really thought I was," I replied. No matter what people said.

Sliding his hands up my arms and to my neck, he gently cradled my face as he kept moving closer. "And here I was thinking you were smart," he whispered, and his lips brushed mine.

Sudden pounding on the door nearly gave me a heart attack. Jumping back, I stared at the front door as the pounding continued, a deafening drumming on steel as someone very aggressively thumped their fist against the surface.

"Who...?" Steve asked, his eyes narrow and his fists clenched. *I feel ya, buddy.*

"I'll just go see who that is," I said, though it was more of a gasp than a full sentence. My heart was still racing by the time I got to the door and peeked through the peephole. The man on the other side was so far from anyone I expected to see that for a second, I just stood there, trying to understand.

But then I realized he would only keep knocking until I opened the door, so I turned the handle and slowly pulled the door open. "Seth?"

My brother stood there as tall as ever, his fist still in the air and his expression the same as mine probably was. "Lissa? What are…" He stiffened, glancing from Brennon's door to Catherine's, and then his confusion morphed into pure, unadulterated anger. "Oh, I'm going to kill him," he growled and shoved his way past me into the apartment. "Ashworth! Brennon Ashworth, you get your sorry ass out here before I come find you so you can explain why you thought it was a good idea to go after my sister."

I clapped my hand over my mouth, but even that couldn't stop me from laughing. I knew Seth was protective, and I loved that about him. But boy did he know how to overreact. "Seth," I said between laughs, "Brennon's not here." And when Seth turned to me, murder in his eyes, I realized Steve had grabbed Captain and was practically hiding behind the fridge.

I'd never laughed so hard in my life. Who needed Pilates when I had men in my life to give me the best ab workout ever?

By the time I could breathe again, Seth had folded his arms and stood in the center of the apartment, his eyes fixed on me so intently that I could only imagine the terror he'd struck into his enemies when he'd gone out on missions with the Special Forces. "Lissa," he said when my laughter finally died. He practically begged for an explanation with that one word.

Closing the door, I walked over to him and wrapped my arms around him in the tightest hug I could manage. "You are literally the best brother in the world," I told him, though he still stood tense and refused to hug me back until I explained. "You have no idea what it means to have someone who isn't my mom be worried about me."

"Your phone call," Seth said, his voice strained. "I tried calling, but it went straight to voicemail. For hours. I *was* worried."

"My phone died," I told him. "I was at the hospital looking after someone, so I couldn't charge it." Guilt shot into my stomach, twisting it in knots again as I thought about what my message must have done to him. "You didn't have to cut your honeymoon short, Seth. I shouldn't have even called."

He finally unfolded his arms so he could wrap them around my shoulders, grunting a little before he said, "Milton sent paparazzi. Catherine's father is nothing if not persistent, and he was hoping to catch some sort of scandal."

Poor Catherine. "How did you know it was him?" I asked.

Seth smirked. "Turns out paparazzi are never very loyal to the people who hire them, so it didn't take a lot of persuasion." That or they were smart enough to know not to mess with the likes of my brother. "Anyway…" Clearing his throat, he glanced around the apartment. "What are you doing over here, Lissa?" he asked, and his eyes landed on Steve in the kitchen. His voice immediately darkened as he kept talking to me. "I saw your stuff over at our place, but you weren't there. So I came over here to see if Brennon had seen you before I went to the police, and here you are."

Here I was. And it was a long explanation for why that was.

"She was helping me," Steve said and stepped forward. He very nearly managed to sound normal, but there was a slight tremor of fear in his voice. He would have been an idiot to not be at least a little intimidated by my brother, though he tried to hide it with a tight smile. "I'm, uh, Steve Evans," he said, holding out his hand. "Brennon's roommate."

Though Seth shook Steve's hand, he pulled his eyebrows together and turned to me as if hoping for some clarification. "I didn't know Ashworth had a roommate," he said after a moment.

I was about to reply when I saw something shift in Steve's expression. He seemed to be sizing Seth up, though I doubted he could see much outside of my brother's sheer bulk. But his uncertain expression changed over the course of a few seconds, so instead of standing there somewhat nervous, now Steve looked like a man with a plan.

I had the sudden mental image of Steve bungee jumping off a bridge in Switzerland without hesitation, and I realized Seth had become a challenge. One Steve was eager to conquer. But what did that mean?

Still holding onto Seth's hand, Steve shook it a little longer than necessary as he said, "You must be the famous Seth Hastings. Lissa has said so much about you. If you don't mind, I'd like to get a good look at you." And then he slammed his palm right into Seth's nose and splayed his fingers across his face.

While Seth tensed and only barely kept himself from attacking, either realizing Steve was blind or simply too stunned to respond, I bit my lip against the laugh that bubbled up inside me. Steve clearly knew he was being ridiculous as he felt around Seth's face, but he was doing a good job of acting entirely serious, as if he could actually get a sense of his features by touching him.

"I can see the family resemblance," Steve said and dropped his hand back to his side, where Captain dutifully waited and gave his fingers a quick lick.

And Seth turned to me, giving me a look that was so easy to read: *Is this guy for real?* he was asking me, but every bit of tension had disappeared from his shoulders despite his slightly concerned expression.

Brennon hadn't been kidding when he said Steve was smart. Now that Seth thought Steve was an absolute idiot, most of his protectiveness had slipped away, leaving the room much calmer than it had been before. And based on the grin Steve was giving me from just beyond Seth's sightline, Seth had reacted exactly as he hoped.

Seth was an incredible big brother, but if his reaction to the idea of me dating Brennon was any indication, he was a bit *too* protective. I was an adult and could make my own decisions, even if they weren't always the best ones. Particularly in this instance—who I fell in love with—I didn't need Seth trying to step in and decide what was best for me. I knew me, and I knew where I could trust my heart.

Steve had just given me a way to find out if this thing between us was lasting, without so much pressure from the outside.

I nearly fell apart, my heart picking up its abnormal pace again for a very different reason than from being startled. He thought he had things all figured out, did he? I would have to prove him wrong before he got too much power, and an idea sparked in my mind out of nowhere. *Try to charm your way through this one, Steve Evans.* "I'm thinking about opening up a restaurant here in San Francisco," I said.

Both men turned to me in surprise, and while Seth pondered the idea with interest, Steve just stared at me like I'd said something absolutely outlandish. He seemed to still be processing my words, as if afraid he had heard them wrong, and that forehead wrinkle of his was back, even if he was having a hard time focusing on me. Clearly I confused the man, a lot, and I was rather proud of myself for being able to throw the likes of Steve Evans off his game.

I grinned. "Steve, of course, would be my head chef."

If only he had been drinking water so I could repeat his earlier spit take. Instead, he just coughed, grabbing the kitchen counter for support as he tried to protect his stitches.

"A restaurant, huh?" Seth asked, his focus on Steve out of the corner of his eye even though he kept his gaze on me. "You've always wanted to do that, haven't you?"

I shrugged. I wanted to help Steve stand upright again, but I knew

I had to ease Seth into this one. Steve may have lessened the pressure considerably, but I had to tread carefully when it came to gentlemen callers. "I think I'm starting to figure out what to do with my life," I said. "I may have freaked out a little prematurely yesterday."

"I don't know much about running a business," Seth said as his smile grew, "but I'm sure Indie and Matthew have a few pointers. That kid has managed to turn a dump into a thriving enterprise in less than six months."

Steve had mostly recovered, but he was looking at me with a hundred different emotions on his face, primarily a mix of confusion, fear, and hope. I needed to talk to him, but to do that I needed to make Seth leave.

"I'll be sure to ask them," I said and put my hand on Seth's back, giving him a gentle nudge toward the door. "By the way, I doubt Matthew would like it if he knew you called him a kid. Isn't he older than you?"

Seth's laugh echoed in the apartment, and luckily he had gotten the hint and was moving toward the door of his own accord. "Only by a few years," he said, giving me a wink. "But that's why I do it. It's fun to watch him try to look angry, but he's like those little dogs who try to be all big and tough but only come across as feisty and adorable."

"You're the worst."

"You love me anyway."

I smiled, watching him cross the hall and feeling a rush of happiness that couldn't fully cover my trepidation about my upcoming conversation with Steve. "You know I do," I said.

As he reached his door, Seth paused and glanced back, though his focus was behind me. Something had just clicked in his mind, it seemed, and he narrowed his eyes as he tried to see past me where Steve was standing. "He was just messing with me, wasn't he?" he growled. He clearly didn't like that idea, and he definitely didn't like it when I grinned in response. "Lissa," he began, but I closed the door before he could say his oncoming threat. He'd be fine, and eventually he would grow to like Steve.

Speaking of… I could feel Steve's gaze even before I turned around, burning into my back as I worked up the courage to look at him again. This was the hard part.

"What was that?" he asked.

I knew what he meant, but I still needed some time to think this through. "That was my dear big brother, Seth Hastings," I said. "I thought you knew that."

"Lissa." He still gripped the counter, his knuckles white. Apparently, he cared a lot about this particular topic of conversation, and I had no intention of causing him more pain than I already had, emotional or physical. He deserved better.

"I meant it," I said. "The restaurant." At least I was pretty sure I did, as long as I could convince myself it wasn't some crazy whim, even if that was exactly what it was. The longer I stood there and imagined it, the wider my smile grew. How had it taken me so long to come to this conclusion when it had been right in front of me all along?

Steve, however, looked almost sick. The dog even nudged his nose against his leg in concern. "Are you insane?" he asked quietly. "You can't waste your time on some childhood dream when I can't even see what I'm cooking."

"Maybe. But you're not the only one who had dreams in the past."

That hit him harder than I expected, and if I hadn't stepped forward and grabbed hold of his arm to keep him steady, I was pretty sure he might have collapsed right there. Helping him to the couch, I sat next to him and gripped his hand.

"Look," I said, "ever since I was a little girl, I wanted to be just like my mom. I spent a lot of nights in her kitchen at whatever restaurant she was working, pretending to do homework while I watched her fly around the kitchen making people happy one plate at a time. But I knew I couldn't afford culinary school, and my mom didn't want me working late hours like I inevitably would. If I wanted to be independent, I had to go with something more secure, so I chose finance. And I've regretted every minute of it."

He shook his head, his eyes on the ground and his eyebrows pulled close together. "Lissa, you have to be logical here."

I *was* being logical. But more importantly, I was also following my gut, something I hadn't had the luxury of doing for a long time. Starting a restaurant just felt right, but no amount of money knowledge or business acumen could make it happen if I didn't have food to serve.

"Steve," I said firmly, and I gently turned his face so he was looking at me. "I'm going to go through with this whether you help me or not because it's what I want to do. But it's been years since I cooked with my mom, and I can't exactly search for world recipes on the internet and get them right. I need your help."

He stared at me as if he couldn't remember the last time he had heard those words directed at him, his eyes wide and a glimmer of hope playing at the corners of his mouth. I nearly had him convinced. Or at least I thought I did, until his shoulders fell and he pulled his hand away from mine. "This is ridiculous," he muttered, and he stood and started pacing, somehow managing to avoid the coffee table without even looking where he was going. "Don't take this the wrong way, but I have a feeling you're not exactly rolling in riches."

"Guilty," I admitted happily.

"And the only reason I'm not completely broke is because Brennon not so secretly adds to my bank account every month and pretends he managed to sell my house for more than it was worth."

"What's your point?" I asked, even though I knew exactly what his point was. I just wanted to hear his argument before I offered mine.

He sighed, pausing just in front of the couch and stuffing his hands into the pocket of his sweatshirt. "Lissa, you can't start a restaurant with no money. And no one in their right mind is going to invest in a blind chef."

"Valid point," I said and got up to join him. "But lucky for us, I happen to have an obscenely wealthy father who's both a little insane and determined to be invested in my life. And I think I just found a way for him to prove that."

Opening his mouth a couple of times, he tried to debate my reasoning but couldn't seem to find anything to say. "Lissa, this is crazy," he muttered. "Why would you choose to bank your future on someone like me?"

Because apparently I knew less about love than a man who didn't even believe it existed. Taking Steve's hand, I shifted a little closer and searched for the right way to explain the warmth in my chest, even if I didn't understand it myself. "For most of my life," I said quietly, "I've been focused on the future. Making a plan and following it to the letter. I have spent so long looking at the destination down the road that I forgot how important it is to pay attention to what is right in front of me." Taking a deep breath, I lifted his hand up to my chest and held it tight against my heart. "I'm willing to take a risk," I said. "Are you?"

Steve frowned, his eyes locked on mine as my heart sank low. But it wasn't an absolute no, and I clung to the hope that there was still a chance I could convince him. He took a deep breath, closing his eyes for a second, and when he looked back at me, his gaze was the most focused I'd ever seen it. Like he saw right into my soul with those ridiculously warm brown eyes.

And then he kissed me.

Well, almost. He got the corner of my mouth, and he breathed a curse and took a step back in embarrassment. I didn't let him get far, grabbing him again and pulling him in for a real kiss. And, oh boy, was it a kiss. Steve didn't need to be able to see to know exactly how to kiss me in a way that left me weak in his arms, hopelessly lost in the best kiss I'd ever had. I closed my eyes and just let myself revel in how perfectly I fit in his arms and how much he managed to say without saying a word. How easily he told me how much he cared for me. Honestly, I wasn't sure if I would ever be able to kiss anyone else.

Not that I wanted to.

I could have stood there forever, but apparently the dog didn't appreciate Steve's attention to me as much as I did, and he jumped up, nearly shoving the pair of us onto the couch.

"Stupid dog," Steve growled and tried to push Captain away so he could keep making me dizzy with happiness.

But the dog was relentless, and I couldn't help but laugh and pull away to get some air. "I have a phone call to make anyway," I said, a little breathless.

Steve managed an impressive glare as he kept trying to stop Captain from knocking him over. "Right this second?" he grumbled.

Maybe I had a couple minutes to spare...

CHAPTER SEVENTEEN

A crash hit my ears, followed by a curse, and I grinned as I pulled picture frames out of a box on the bed. I knew what would come next, and sure enough, an endless stream of expletives slowly grew louder as Steve made his way down the hallway toward my bedroom.

"Remind me why I can't move that coffee table before I no longer have any shins," he said as soon as he was safely inside the room. It took him a second, but he found me on the far side of the bed and immediately wrapped his arms around me from behind.

Given how well I fit in his hold from the start, I hadn't been sure how I would feel about him gaining weight. But three months of hearty meals and even some time at the gym had definitely added to his bulk in a good way, and I had yet to find a downside to the change. "Feng shui," I said and burrowed myself a little deeper into his arms. Now I understood how Catherine felt every time she got lost in Seth's embrace, and I couldn't blame her for doing it as often as possible.

"You don't believe in feng shui," he replied and pulled a frame out of my hand to hold it closer to his face. "Okay, please tell me this is a picture of you as an awkward teenager and not a photo of a llama."

"Ouch." I twisted around and tried to grab the picture out of his hand, but he easily held it up and just out of reach. Though he definitely couldn't see my high school graduation photo from that high up, he still pretended to examine it carefully as he ignored my attempts to pull his arm down to retrieve the picture. So there was one downside to him doubling his muscle weight...

"Perm was a good look for you," he said.

"You don't even know what a perm is," I argued and jumped, barely managing to grasp the picture and tear it out of his hand.

"I'm pretty sure any look is a good look for you, Liss."

I rolled my eyes. "Says the guy who couldn't tell if that was a picture of me or a llama."

"If it helps," he said with a grin, "you don't look like a llama now."

I thought about scowling at him, but judging by the way he was focusing more on my nose than my eyes, I figured he couldn't really see my expression. "That's not as flattering as you seem to think it is," I told him and slipped out from under his arm. "Where are Seth and Catherine?"

Steve grabbed my elbow before I could get out the door. "Where do you think you're going?" he growled, and then he pulled me back into his arms and kissed me quite thoroughly.

It took me a second to remember what I'd asked him, and if he hadn't kept his arm around my waist, I probably would have fallen over. "That..." *Focus, Lissa.* He already suspected he could disarm me with one of his kisses, and I didn't need him to know it was absolutely true. "That wasn't an answer."

He smirked, a little too self-aware. "They're on their way up," he said.

As if on cue, my front door opened and a shout echoed through my new apartment: "Lissa! The menus look *amazing!* You have to come see."

My stomach dropped, and before I could even start hyperventilating, Steve took my hand and gave it a squeeze. "Try not to freak out," he said then headed out to greet my brother and sister-in-law.

I took a steadying breath. I hadn't had a lot of free time the last few months, busy planning my restaurant and getting everything ready, but things were happening too fast. If the menus were ready, it meant we only had to finish the remodel of the venue. And then it was make or break time, and I had no idea if this would even succeed. What did I know about running a restaurant?

I needed one more minute to ground myself in the reality that was my life. Something to give me the strength to go out there and face such a big unknown.

My fingers shaking a little, I pulled one more photo from the box and smiled at it. It was my absolute favorite picture, even if it was a little out of focus and my right ear was cut out of the shot. Steve had insisted on taking it himself. It was Christmas at Lanna and Adam's house, just a couple of weeks after that first time he kissed me. He took the photo of us two seconds before he told me he loved me.

"You happen to like that picture, don't you?"

I turned, grinning at Steve where he leaned against the door frame with his hands in his pockets. He probably hadn't even made it two steps before turning around and coming back to watch me. Setting the photo next to my bed, I crossed the room slowly and took his hand before kissing his cheek. "I happen to like it very much," I told him, my voice wavering against my will.

His eyes searched my face, a little wrinkle appearing between his eyebrows as his frustration grew because he couldn't see my expression. "Are you happy?" he asked.

What kind of a bone-headed question was that? "Of course I'm happy," I said. "I have a new apartment, a perfect family, a father who amazingly has yet to let me down. And I have you." I slid my hands up to his neck, rising up on my toes and touching my lips to his.

"Do you happen to like me too?" he whispered, the line in his forehead growing.

I smiled and deepened my kiss. "I happen to love you," I said.

"Good, because I happen to love you too. Everything's going to work out." He grabbed my hand, kissing my palm before threading our fingers together. "I promise."

The second we stepped into the living room, Seth coughed and muttered, "Remember what I told you, Evans."

I turned to Steve in alarm, wondering what Seth could have possibly told him without me knowing about it, but Steve put on an impressively smug expression. "I'm not afraid of you, Hastings," he said.

Seth narrowed his eyes. "Maybe if you could actually see me you would be."

"Will you two idiots stop so Lissa can look at these?" Catherine said, strategically stepping in between the two of them and holding out a laminated sheet of paper to me. "Lanna did an incredible job on these," she told me with a grin.

As I'd quickly discovered, Catherine's cousin had an impressively artistic eye, and without her, my menus would have been plain black text on white background. Instead, she'd created something both functional and beautiful, adding influences from every country the dishes came from.

"They're perfect," I breathed. "Steve, I wish you could see these."

He was still in a bit of a stare-down with Seth, but he smiled and replied, "I'll trust your judgment, my love, as long as your brother doesn't kill me first."

"Seth," Catherine warned.

My brother slowly unclenched his fists and gave me a pained look. He'd definitely gotten better over the last couple of months, but Seth wasn't fully okay with the idea of me dating someone, particularly an "imbecile" like Steve. He told me so often. After getting the full story of my little relationship with Brennon and learning about Steve's fiancée and her possible connection to us, he'd gotten even more protective, no matter how many times I told him he didn't have a say in my relationships. I hadn't thought that was possible until Catherine told me about the moment she had to drag Seth into their apartment after he cornered Steve in the hallway. Apparently, Steve had made it a habit to annoy my brother as often as he possibly could and was particularly good at playing the fool, something Seth didn't much appreciate.

Eventually Seth would figure out what I had, and he would realize there were few men better than Steve Evans. I was most definitely becoming convinced there was no one better for me in particular.

He makes me happy, I tried to tell Seth with my gaze. Honestly, what more could he want for me?

"And now that you've seen the menus," Catherine said, taking Seth's hand and practically forcing him to relax a little, "am I allowed to know what's in the Tupperware? I could smell it the whole drive over from Steve's place."

"It's food," Steve said without looking away from Seth.

"You're an idiot," Seth muttered and pinched the bridge of his nose, as if Steve's very presence was giving him a migraine. Either Steve had been hard at work during the drive over, or Seth's tolerance was incredibly low today.

I rolled my eyes. "It's sampling for Matthew and Indie," I explained, meeting Catherine's eye and sharing a grin. At least she agreed with me—our men were a little ridiculous. "They're considering Steve to cater their wedding and are coming over for a taste testing."

"Good," Catherine said. "I know Lanna loves her little caterer, Josh, but the guy's food hasn't changed in half a decade. He needs to spice it up a bit. What country are they thinking?" she asked Steve.

"Italy," he replied. "Or Greece."

I had no idea why Seth smirked about Greece or why Indie and Matthew were considering Greek in the first place, but the Italian made sense. Indie's first husband was Italian, and Matthew was impressively thoughtful and made sure she didn't have to forget her first love.

Just as I was about to ask Seth why he thought Greek was funny, Indie herself opened the door with a knock and grinned. "I could smell it from the hallway," she said eagerly, stepping over to Steve. "I'm not sure I even have to taste it to know you're hired."

Matthew was just behind her, and it only took him a second to take in the scene before he started laughing. "Relax, Seth," he said, joining his fiancée. He, at least, had taken a liking to Steve even before I had, and the pair of them had become quick friends. Leaning close to Steve, Matthew muttered something then grinned.

Steve immediately wrapped his arm around my waist, pulling me close and touching his lips to my neck. "Can't help it," he whispered into my ear as I shivered.

Seth growled from the other side of our little circle.

Though I was tempted to join in on Steve's fun, I figured I probably shouldn't push my brother to his limit. At least not tonight. "Be nice," I told Steve just as my phone started buzzing. I glanced at the ID for only a second before I answered: "Hi, Dad."

"Did the menus come?"

I smiled and pulled away from Steve's hold so I could hear Gordon over the chatter of my family. "They came," I confirmed, "and they look amazing."

"I was worried about that Munroe girl, but after that first sample she sent me, I knew you'd found someone worthy of the job. How's the space looking?" He sounded both excited and nervous, and I knew it was hard for him to be so far away while everything was happening. His work with the Department of Homeland Security had kept him on the East Coast for the last two months, but that hadn't stopped him from helping wherever he could with the restaurant.

"They were putting in the floors this morning," I said, and my heart started racing again. Opening day was rapidly approaching.

"I ordered some higher quality chairs," Gordon said. "Same style, better manufacturer. They should be there next week."

"Thanks, Dad." It still felt weird calling him that, but he had been adamant that I say nothing else. "You've been amazing through all of this."

He was quiet for a moment, and when he spoke again, I could hear the emotion in his voice. "I told you," he said. "I really mean to be a part of your life. I'm glad you let me in."

Surprisingly, "Me too," I said.

"Send me pictures tomorrow. I want to make sure they're not cutting any corners with that tile work."

"Sure thing."

"I…" He paused. "Thanks, Lissa." He hung up the phone, but I kept it pressed to my ear for a moment. He was close. For a man who had spent so long denying my existence, it was a miracle he could even try to say how much he cared.

In a matter of a few months, I had gone from almost alone to having a family. A huge family. My mom was planning on coming out with her husband for the restaurant's opening day, and Gordon—Dad— had been monumentally essential in getting me to this point with the restaurant. Without him, I couldn't have even considered the idea. Though Lanna was pregnant enough with her second child that she was trying to take it easy, she had put so much time and effort into the designing of the menus and the restaurant's decor that I had considered naming a dish after her. Seth and Catherine had found me a place to stay until I could find an apartment near the restaurant, and though Seth wasn't the biggest fan of Steve as my boyfriend, he'd still supported the idea of him being my head chef and was always willing to taste test food if Brennon wasn't around. Matthew had been Steve's personal chauffeur for weeks and helped him practice cooking without seeing, while Indie had spent hours every evening walking me through the process of owning and running a business.

And as I stood there in my little apartment, I could hardly choke back tears as I watched them all gathered around the table. Catherine smiled as she scooped out portions of everything Steve had made that afternoon. Seth—bless his heart—couldn't help but match her expression no matter how much he wanted to keep glaring at Steve. Matthew talked with Steve about where he should take Indie on their honeymoon, while Indie kept glancing at her engagement ring in between bites of food and smiling to herself.

I'd honestly never thought I would have something like this. My whole life it had been Mom and me, and I knew I wasn't destined for love. Of any kind. And yet…

Steve turned, searching me out as if he knew something was wrong.

He always knew. Muttering something to Matthew, he got to his feet and came to my side, the crease between his eyebrows deep. "Tell me," he said, worry in his low voice.

But I smiled, brushing away my tears and falling into his hold. The future was so uncertain, and there were so many things I didn't have an answer to. I was glad I didn't have to be uncertain about him. "Sometimes I wonder when I'm going to wake up and realize all of this is a dream," I admitted.

His arms pulled me tighter. "Good dream or bad dream?" he asked.

"Good," I said and rested my head on his shoulder, wishing I could stay there forever instead of facing the unpredictable future. But I meant what I said. Everything about my life was incredible, particularly when it came to Steve. "Definitely good."

Gently pressing his lips against my forehead, he took a deep breath that made me smile because it meant he was healthy and whole. "Then I hope you never wake up," he said, "because I refuse to give you up."

"Promise?"

"Would I ever lie to you?"

That, at least, I did have an answer for: "No. You wouldn't."

He pulled away just enough to look into my eyes, and I was pretty sure he could see everything inside my head and my heart. "No matter what happens, Lissa," he said, "I love you. Nothing is going to change that."

And I believed him.

The End

Special sneak peek of Book 5 in the Simple Love Series,

As Long as You Love Me

EXCERPT FROM *AS LONG AS YOU LOVE ME*

In general, my life was pretty simple. Simplicity provided room for predictability, and if I could anticipate what might happen, I was never caught off guard. If I was never caught off guard, well, I never got hurt. Logically, it wasn't the best way to live life, but I had survived the last fifteen years with that philosophy, and I planned to keep it up. Why would I change when it worked? *If it ain't broke, don't fix it.*

"You're in a mood today."

I looked up from my computer screen, realizing I had been staring at it for too long and getting lost in thought while the page refreshed. I would have to talk to Jake about our internet problems, because it was really starting to get ridiculous. Eight seconds to load a spreadsheet? At least I was mostly awake now.

"Sorry," I said and gave Colin Donovan a smile. "Long week." *Long night, more like,* but I knew how he would take that.

Stop living such a wild life, he would say, and we would laugh a little because Donovan went out with people even less often than I did, though he had a good reason for staying at home.

He was one of my oldest clients, thankfully, so he'd seen me at my good and bad and simply gave me a half-smile that told me he understood. Donovan was one of the few exceptions to my general rule about never meeting with clients in person. Over the years, he had become one of the most predictable people I knew, so I didn't have to wonder what he might do or say. He was here because he was going on vacation for the bulk of the summer, just like he did every year. He wanted to make sure I had everything in order with his funds so he didn't come back any poorer than when he left.

I wanted to stop thinking about Molly, because she was seriously messing with my head and making my job harder than it needed to be. How was it she managed to disrupt my life even when I hadn't seen her in years? I could still see her as she was in my dream, biting the end of her pencil as she sprawled across my floor and did her quiz. Just like when we were teens.

I took a quick glance at Donovan's file now that it had loaded, though I already knew it well, and I jumped right into explaining my plans for the next couple of months. It wasn't anything different from what I'd been doing the last couple of years, and Colin wasn't any more worried than he usually was. He trusted me to take care of his money, just like all my clients did.

Predictable. Logical. Simple.

Everything my dream last night *wasn't*.

"I'll have my phone on me," Donovan assured me as he left, though the odds of me needing to call him were slim to none.

Thankfully, the meeting restored a bit of balance to my day, and I had a feeling things would be better from here on out. Now that things were more or less back to normal, I settled more comfortably in my chair and went to work. This, alone in my office with nothing but money and spreadsheets to keep me company, was where I could be completely myself.

As usual, Jake had lunch on my desk almost the instant I realized I was hungry, and I looked up at him wondering how I could have found someone so perfect. "You know me too well," I said, though I really wanted to tell him he was sent from heaven.

Jake laughed as he grabbed a water bottle from his back pocket and tossed it to me. "Yeah," he agreed. "I know you're always hungry."

"I'm not always…" But I stopped myself because he was right. It was the curse of spending the last couple of years living with the man who was the head chef of one of San Francisco's most popular restaurants. Steve Evans was a genius on a stove, and he'd had to practice before his restaurant opened. A lot. I had to admit I had gotten used to eating his attempts, which were always amazing, and I definitely missed that perk. My stomach missed it. Weekly family dinners with the Davenports were not enough to curb my cravings for the man's food.

"Do I pay you enough?" I asked Jake, already knowing the answer.

"Nope," he said, and then he was out the door and back at his desk.

I'd have to bring that up at the next staff meeting, since I had a feeling I wasn't the only guy at *Bay Bridge Investments* who relied heavily on his assistant. I only had so many Warriors tickets to give him before he realized his talents were worth more for him to leave than to stay and help keep my life on a schedule.

The afternoon passed quickly, as it always did, and the stock market didn't do anything I hadn't predicted. One company I had invested in on behalf of multiple clients had suddenly dropped in value over the weekend when the CEO was caught siphoning funds, but I had expected that after meeting the guy a month ago and had sold last week. Another stock had soared, a start-up that caught the attention of the internet with a well-made commercial. Again, I had anticipated this the moment I found the video last week and had already purchased a significant number of shares. Work, as always, was gloriously predictable.

"And this is why you love what you do," I said to myself.

Around six, I was back to singing that stupid Backstreet Boys song when Jake knocked on my office door, probably to bring in my dinner, so I called out for him to enter and kept singing.

"Interesting choice," said a man who wasn't Jake.

I jumped to my feet the moment I recognized Jefferson, one of the partners of our firm. I'd spoken to the guy a few times, but he rarely came down to talk to us brokers because he was too busy building up the company and schmoozing new clients. Unlike me, Jefferson was a people person and loved being out and about, chatting and golfing and going out to lunch with people. Even now, he looked like he'd just come off a coastline cruise, which I'd heard was one of his favorite things. His thick silver hair was windswept and enviable.

"Mr. Jefferson," I said quickly and held out my hand for him to shake. My office suddenly felt sweltering, and I desperately hoped my hand wasn't sweaty.

Jefferson's handshake was firm, and he took to examining my office rather than me as he shook. "How long have you been here, Ashworth?" he asked after a moment.

I had to count back the years to answer Jefferson's question, so he probably thought I was a bit slow. "Uh, eleven years, sir."

"Eleven years," he repeated, his eyebrows high. "That's a long time."

I had no idea what he meant by that. "Uh. Yeah. It's a good company."

He started wandering my small office, looking at the few things I had on my shelves. Books and files, mainly, but I had a picture of my parents by the door, as well as a photo of Steve and me just after we graduated Stanford next to my little fern that sat in the window. "You like it here?" he asked, touching one of the fern leaves.

"Of course," I said, though I was a little worried I would start singing out loud again if that song didn't stop playing in my head. I was so focused on Jefferson being here that I could barely focus on holding my tongue. But was he really asking if I liked my job? I was pretty sure I had succeeded in never making anyone suspect that I didn't. I wanted to be predictable, after all.

"So why haven't you tried to become a partner?"

Never mind needing to hold my tongue. My words caught in my throat, and I stood there feeling like I was brand new to the company and had no idea what I was doing. Partner? That had been my goal from the beginning, but I figured I was simply mediocre, since no one had ever brought it up with me. Until now, at least. "Sir?" It was the only word that I could think of that wasn't absolute nonsense.

Jefferson grimaced as he settled in the chair opposite my desk and gestured for me to sit as well. "Janice was right," he muttered. "You are ridiculously proper, aren't you?"

The song was playing in my head again, and I got distracted enough that I wasn't sure what he said at first. "Uh."

The grimace turned into an amused smile. "Relax, Ashworth. You're not in trouble."

I couldn't remember the next line of the song. And I didn't know what to say. I tried to take a deep breath, hoping that would knock some sense into me that didn't involve Nick Carter's voice, but everything about this impromptu meeting was too confusing. I just ended up giving myself chest pains as I sat there. "I didn't think I was," I managed to get out at the same time my head jumped back to the chorus of the song. "I'm just... I'm not sure what you're getting at. Sir," I added, for good measure.

Jefferson let out a chuckle and picked up a book I'd left on my desk with the intent to read but had never given myself the time. It had sat there for months. *The 7 Habits of Highly Effective People*. It was one of

Steve's favorites, but I hadn't even opened it after he and Lissa gave it to me for my birthday a couple months before.

I was pretty sure they'd just given me the exact copy I already owned, since it had the same mark on the long edge of the pages, but whatever. I wasn't going to read it anyway.

Even with interesting books, reading made it way too easy to get lost in my thoughts lately. *Curse you for throwing off my equilibrium, Lissa.* She didn't even know she'd done it. She was almost as bad as Molly.

And still the Backstreet Boys kept singing.

"Shut up," I growled under my breath.

"You have the best numbers in the entire company," Jefferson said, thankfully distracted as he browsed the book. "You're always here early, always leave late, and I can't even begin to tell you how many potential clients have heard about you and want you as their broker."

The office temperature rose again. "Oh," I said, which sounded ridiculous but was a whole lot better than any of the crooning lyrics running through my head. I decided I should probably say something else, though. "Uh, thank you."

"Which brings me back to the question: Why haven't you tried to make partner?"

Did he really expect me to have an answer to that? Because I didn't. Yes, I wanted to become a partner and have some say in the workings of the firm. Yes, I worked harder than I should in the hopes my efforts would be noticed. But did he want me to say that? To tell him that he and the other company head had spent the last eleven years basically unaware that I existed? *How about I guilt you into giving me the job?*

He looked up at me, making eye contact for the first time. He looked older than I remembered, though I was pretty sure he couldn't have been more than fifty. Only fifteen years at most separated us, but I felt like we were worlds apart. Kort Jefferson knew exactly what he was doing with his life and what he wanted to have happen and how to reach his goals without worrying about stepping on other people's toes or saying the wrong things. He was confident and charismatic and had everything he could possibly want.

And I…

"You seem like a good kid," he said, his eyebrows pulling together as my silence continued, "but you can't be afraid to go for what you want. Initiative is more powerful than most people realize."

"Yes," I said a little too quickly. *Smooth.* "I mean, I'll keep that in mind."

He smiled a bit as he rose to his feet and gave my office another little examination. "You aren't big into stuff, are you, Ashworth?" he said.

"I don't see the point of holding onto things," I said without hesitation. That I did have a response for, though I kept the second half to myself: *Everything inevitably goes away.* I had learned that lesson early on in life.

My comment made his smile widen, and he said, "Sounds like you found the right business," as he headed for the door. "Money never hangs around for long. I'll see you around, Ashworth."

It was for that exact reason I had become a stock broker. Compared to dealing with people, the stock market was blissfully predictable.

As soon as Jefferson was gone, the last couple of minutes seemed to rush into me and knock me down into my chair. Had he just said...? I had pretty much decided becoming a partner was out of the question, which was fine. I knew my place, and I was good at what I did. Not everyone could claim that. But Jefferson seemed to want me doing more, which was so far from what I expected that I felt pretty dizzy as I sat there.

Or maybe that was because I was hungry.

Reaching across my relatively empty desk, I tapped the intercom button on my phone and said, "Jake?"

"Dinner's on its way, Brennon," he replied immediately.

I definitely didn't pay the kid enough. And until he started working for me three years earlier, I hadn't realized just how valuable it was to have an assistant who recognized the benefit of predictability, just like I had.

Without really meaning to, I muttered some lyrics out loud, though the song was long gone, replaced with a million questions I didn't have answers for.

And I really didn't like that.

ABOUT THE AUTHOR

Dana LeCheminant has been telling stories since she was old enough to know what stories were. After spending most of her childhood reading everything she could get her hands on, she eventually realized she could write her own books too, and since then she always has plots brewing and characters clamoring to be next to have their stories told. A lover of all things outdoors, she finds inspiration while hiking the remote Utah backcountry and cruising down rivers. Until her endless imagination runs dry, she will always have another story to tell.

CPSIA information can be obtained
at www.ICGtesting.com
Printed in the USA
LVHW090900150720
660701LV00004B/333